Bar Whores

By

Kenneth M. Kielty

Contents

Blue Moon

Never a clear reason why our family left the comforts of Floral Park, New York, that October. We moved to a seventy-acre farm in the Catskill Mountains. Our mother claimed it was because she wanted us kids to live close to nature, to raise animals on a real farm. Our father argued it was because my mother wanted a place for our latest family acquisition, a dog. He showed up in our yard one day. We called him Buck.

The mailman claimed to know dogs and declared this black collie of ours a very special breed, a Nova Scotia sheepdog to be exact. He went on to explain these dogs could only thrive in wide-open spaces, thus our farm was ideal. Whenever the question of why we moved came up, our father blamed it on the dog.

The real reason was simple. Our parents hated—no, loathed each other, needed to escape the train wreck they tried to pass off as marriage.

In the mid-fifties Catholics didn't get divorces—we moved instead. Father stayed on Long Island and continued to work at Sperry Gyroscope in Great Neck.

Mom enjoyed her freedom from the dread associated with being married to what she called "that stinking, rotten, drunken Irishman."

Upstate meant many changes for the family. We had no idea what rural life would bring. No longer able to run to the A&P Supermarket two houses up from us on Jericho Turnpike. No longer a walk away from Saint Hedwig Catholic Grade School, visible from our front porch.

We came to resent our new country school, an hour-long bus ride over the dusty back roads of Green County. The closest store was three miles away.

No supermarket like our beloved A&P, where the butcher flirted with our mother. Instead, we had a general store that sold everything from butter to guns.

To replenish our food supply, we either caught a taxicab or walked the three miles there and three miles back.

Father left mother with a 1946 Plymouth stick shift. She didn't have a driver's license. Never learned how to drive a car, let alone a stick shift.

The A&P was replaced by the steely-eyed Dutch family that ran their new general store in the village close to our farm. The "Dutchmen," as they were known, were suspicious of us city folk. When our family arrived at the store—five kids, plus mother—a clerk felt prompted to follow us around in case we tried to steal candy or ice cream. We felt like a swarm of gypsies.

Back on Long Island, our mother had never learned to manage a household. Father sent her forty dollars a week. He presumed that covered the groceries, utilities, and whatever else came up. Mom didn't know enough to tell him otherwise.

Our new home, a giant single-floor farmhouse, had about ten rooms, including six bedrooms. The sole source of heat was a single kerosene stove in the middle of the house. This area became our living room, dining room, and recreation area. My two sisters and mother had one bedroom. Me and my two brothers the other. The additional four bedrooms were too cold, so we seldom ventured in. Our neighbors told us the farmer, the previous owner, had had three wives, who all died in various back bedrooms. An ancient hospital bed still present in the farthest room was all the evidence we needed to confirm the story.

As Catholics, we attended Catholic schools all our lives up to the move. In our new small town, we entered public school. Being city folks in a conservative Protestant area, we weren't met with warmth and acceptance by the staff or students.

One of my first encounters with my new third grade teacher, Mrs. Engle, came with the recital of the official state school prayer.

"Young man, why are you not praying with the rest of us?" she asked, singling me out. It seemed I had a simple enough excuse—as a Catholic, I considered it a Protestant prayer and refused to recite it. So much for voluntary prayers. My assignment for the next day: lead the class in the official New York State School Prayer, which, to the best of my memory, went something like

> Almighty God, we acknowledge our
> dependence upon thee and beg thy blessings
> upon us, our parents, and our teachers. Amen.

I was overwhelmed with personal pleasure when, years later as an undergraduate, I learned the US Supreme Court case of Engle vs. Vitale outlawed the New York State School Prayer. No relationship to the teacher, of course, but I found my personal "vengeance is mine, so sayeth the Lord" moment deeply gratifying.

Upon our move to the new house, a team of movers from Long Island took it upon themselves to turn on the water pump that supplied water from our artesian well with no thought to prime the pump. It burnt out within the hour.

We lived for nine months without running water. Water we needed to wash ourselves, our clothes, and flush toilets had to be hauled in from the well in five-gallon buckets. We retrieved it from the milk house in the barn. Late spring, father enlisted the expertise of a plumber. The farmhouse was a mix of stone and stucco. It gave off an unusual musty odor that offended the nostrils upon entrance. This, accompanied by the stench of the kerosene stove and un-flushed toilets, gave each child a unique stink we carried with us. We sat together on the bus alone, outcasts.

We lasted three years upstate before we limped back to Long Island, a new town, new school. Our parents still fought and liberally threatened the D-word when their arguments got hot.

Mom took a trip to Mexico to get a divorce. New York's strict divorce laws at the time dictated the only justifiable reason for divorce as adultery. Even though both parents probably qualified, the idea they'd have to admit in front of a judge that they'd sinned didn't appeal to either of them.

The trip was a disaster from the start. Mom actually took a bus from the Port Authority in Manhattan all the way to Texas. She called home to check on us, walked away from the phone booth, and left her wallet, identification, and her divorce money for some lucky vagrant. She called home collect.

"What are you doing in Texas? I thought you were visiting your Aunt Mae in Florida."

Humiliated, she had to ask dad to wire her money so she could get home to New York.

We lasted a year and a half on Long Island before we took off again for the solace of upstate New York, the alleged tranquility of rural life.

The first time we had lived upstate, we managed to accumulate a paltry menagerie of animals on our small seventy-acre farm. Goats, pigs, geese, ducks, and a lone horse ran wild, as did we, with our seven dogs.

To leave animals meant one thing—we had to call the butcher shop who'd help us gather the animals for their last ride. The horse we boarded out, but the switch from free range to fixed captivity proved more than our poor mare could bear. The new keepers tied her up with a slipknot and she choked herself to death.

Now, as older kids, we petitioned our mother to spare us the animals this time this time around. The dogs we kept.

Compared to Long Island with our parents' constant quarrels, we found upstate living peaceful, almost boring.

Father made occasional trips to visit us and harass our mother. His visits brought mixed emotions. The arguments and threats escalated with his consumption of beer and whiskey. On the other hand, dad's visits meant a chance to eat out. Our only option, dad's choice: pizza at the Blue Moon Bar and Restaurant.

Although mom learned to drive, she never rode up front with my father in the car. Instead, she sat in the back seat with us kids. My saccharine family of seven headed off to the Blue Moon for pizza and a show. His sadistic rants and abuses ratcheted up with each drink.

The last time I remember going to the Blue Moon as a family was in 1961. I was almost an eighth grader, and the occasion for the trip was to celebrate our parents' divorce. They managed to convince the great state of Alabama their marriage was "irreconcilably broken." It worked. Father had the papers drawn; mom signed them. After "seventeen years of hell," as she repeated so often, the marriage was over.

What also made this trip unusual was that Mother insisted on driving to the Blue Moon. She asked my older sister to sit between her and her ex-husband.

The Blue Moon, three miles from our house, had a ball field on the property filled with players from various boarding houses and resorts. When we first moved to the Catskills, any given summer brought hundreds of people gathered to defend the honor of their favorite summer retreat.

The favorite teams were those who had strong ethnic roots. When the Irishmen from East Durham came to play the Italians, the Blue Moon took on the excitement of Yankee Stadium. The Italians often won. The Irish were too drunk to make it past the seventh inning.

A few years earlier, our father had tried his hand at ball with the Irish team. He lasted a few innings. Took a beer break and never returned.

My younger brother and I often walked to the field on weekends to watch the games. We shagged foul balls or searched the marsh beyond the home run fence for lost balls. Found balls fetched a quarter. When good teams played, we made a few dollars—sometimes enough for a cheese pizza.

Now, the last weekend of the summer of 1961, the field stood empty. The parking lot at the Blue Moon held only a few cars, the glory of the Catskills had faded. Families vacationed in other destinations. The smell of clean air, the taste of fresh food, seemed to have lost its appeal to city folks.

Mother hated the Blue Moon, the place that fueled my father's fury. On a few occasions after family gatherings, the New York State Highway Patrol was called to our humble farm to break up a knock-down drag-out between Mom and Dad—Mother the one knocked down and dragged out, never our father.

Oftentimes, our father dropped us off at home after our Blue Moon experiences. He'd tell us he had business to take care of. Mother would explain, once he was safely out the door, that he headed back to the Blue Moon to meet up with one of those hussy waitresses.

We learned early on such words as hussy, tramp, and the killer of all names, whore. Mother used whore sparingly, only when convinced the name fit the woman who, indeed, was one of our father's conquests.

One night still remains a family classic. Home from the Blue Moon, Dad made an announcement he had additional business that needed his immediate attention. Mother pleaded he was too drunk to drive, pointing out he'd barely made it home that night. If he went out he would probably kill himself along with a car full of other people. He ignored her pleas and left the house.

As he pulled out of the driveway, my mother began screaming at us kids. "Pray that your stinking rotten father drives off into a ditch and kills himself. Pray that he crashes his car." The five of us looked on as she continued her tirade against our father.

The only thing to quiet her was when the front door opened and Dad staggered in asking for a towel. His forehead was covered with blood. My older sister raced to the bathroom to retrieve a towel. Before my father dabbed the gash on his wound he looked at the towel and made sure it was clean.

The twins began to cry. My older brother asked, "What happened?"

My father's reply, immortalized in the archives of ridiculous statements: "Yeah, I must have slipped on the ice and the car went into a ditch." It was May.

Mother's retort also makes the list of famous family quotes. "God answered my prayers, you stinking rotten bastard."

So life went on in Green County for our family. The occasional weekends our father visited became fewer, and with the divorce, we accepted his visits would cease. This trip would probably be our last as a full family to the Blue Moon.

For me, the last trip held a memory of my father that lasted a lifetime.

George, the bartender, greeted our tribe in his usual fashion: a cold stare and curled lip below his thick black mustache.

Try as he might, our father, considered by strangers to be a real talker and have a winning personality, could never hook George into a conversation. Thus, in our household George simply became "The Stiff" at the Blue Moon.

Despite George's dark disposition, the waitresses were genuinely pleased when my father entered with his family in tow, all smiles and wiggles.

Over the years, a pattern to our madness had evolved in our visits to the Blue Moon. My father always entered first. He waved toward the bar. George ignored all of us. The waitress on duty recognized Dad and called out to him by some nickname he'd earned on another occasion.

My older brother and our father shared the same name. When the waitresses said something to our father, our older brother would answer. This went on two or three times before the slap came fast and hard against my brother's face.

Dad never referred to his eldest by name. "The Gom" was his favorite name for him, often modified to "Goddamn Gom" or something more sentimental like "Shit for Brains."

Whenever the God word came out of Father's mouth, Mother, up and ready for battle, chided him for using "God's name in vain."

The family's seating arrangement was always the same. Our father and the three boys at one table. Mother and the two girls at another. If a waitress suggested we all sit together, Father would tell her separate tables kept peace between the children.

George's revulsion of our family had started years back.

Our farmhouse's never-ending plumbing issues left us without running water for weeks, sometimes months at a time.

A visit to the Blue Moon inevitably transpired on one of Father's infrequent visits from the city. The command of "washing up" meant we'd use the bar bathroom to take our sponge baths. Hot water in the sink, we'd strip to our waists, soap up, rinse, and dry off with paper towels.

George caught us a few times. Never said a word, just shook his head in disgust and sent the dishwasher in to mop up after us.

Our humiliation never seemed to phase our father.

This last night as a family at the Blue Moon, we had Bernie as our waitress. We all knew her as Dad's favorite. Her daughter, Tammy, was a classmate of mine.

Tammy schooled me on several occasions with regard to her mother and my father's good friendship, accompanied by a smirk and wink. Tammy was the class whore and wore the title proudly.

She claimed to have lost her virginity to an eighth-grade boy when she was in sixth grade. By eighth grade, Tammy had a steady flow of high school boys who patronized her house while her mom worked.

Tonight, Bernie approached our table and greeted our father with one of her pet names. My older brother kept silent, clear she addressed our father, not him.

"How's my crazy Irish rose man doing this evening?" She stood in front of our table, cigarette dangling from the corner of her mouth. I never remember her without a smoke, either in her mouth or between her fingers. As she took our order she placed the cancer stick on the left side of her mouth, and it bobbed up and down with every word. She started out, hands on hips, a casual conversation. But as she became more animated, her cigarette became more of a conductor's baton. Smoke fogged her face as her gravelly voice waxed on; her listeners couldn't focus on anything but the dancing cigarette in her mouth.

Bernie's light pink nylon waitress dress appeared to be a few sizes too small. Her uniform zipped up the front like many of the dresses she wore to work at the Blue Moon. Mother observed the zipper appeared to lower itself over the course of dinner, especially as she waited on our father's table. Two white breasts with a dark valley between revealed themselves as the night wore on. Her long black hair rested on the sides of her bulging bosoms like a frame. The boys in the family all shared a fondness for Bernie's knockers. We dared not linger too long in our stares, however, lest mother noticed.

Like many women in the Catskills, Bernie worked two jobs in the summer, a chambermaid for one of the local boarding houses in Oak Hill and her waitress job at the bar. She started her typical day at six in the morning, off at two, then over to the Blue Moon by five where she worked until eleven. From Memorial Day to Labor Day Bernie worked her grueling schedule.

The winter months brought visits to the state unemployment office. She picked up cash jobs where she could find them.

Bernie and Tammy took off for Florida in the winter. After her husband divorced her, she lost the use of the in-laws' home. Tammy appreciated enrollment in one school for a whole year. She she said she got to know the boys better.

Such was the life of Catskill women in the early sixties.

Bernie only tended Mom's table to deliver the food and drinks. Dad placed all the orders. The girls got a small cheese pizza and one soda each. Our table got a large sausage with extra cheese and one soda a piece. Our mother nibbled on crust the girls left on their plates.

Fleischmann's whiskeys and beer chasers kept Bernie busy all night. "My goodness, where do you put all those drinks?" she said at least four times each evening. Once we polished off the pizza, we sat quietly while Dad downed his drinks.

Father had few talents. Diagnosed with polio as a child, his right arm was slightly deformed and smaller than his left. Sports wasn't something he excelled at, but he could sing. The term *Irish tenor* is used loosely to describe any Irishman with a hint of vocal talent.

Five or six shots of whiskey, followed by chasers, and then the waitress on duty usually coaxed him to play the piano and sing. His piano ability was barely adequate as he couldn't read music. He played by ear. Even George stopped what he was doing to listen to a few bars of each song. The songs were always Irish. When Dad struggled to play the music, he sang a cappella. People told him he should have been a professional singer. Some asked if he'd made any records.

When people hear Irish ballads, it evokes their emotions. Thoughts of Ireland, a long dead parent, a lost love. I hear Irish songs and see cheap red-and-white-checkered table cloths on the tables of the Blue Moon complete with the wicker Chianti bottles with melted candle wax burrowed between glass and wicker.

No Blue Moon dinner was complete without a confrontation. After his sixth or seventh drink this night, Dad noticed our older brother had worn his new school clothes. For some reason, new school clothes weren't to be worn anywhere but school. I never figured out the old man's logic, but it was one of his rules and we lived by it.

Mother never questioned this rule. Father and his mother bought most of our clothes, so if Mom wanted to criticize "the rule," then quite possibly our supply of school, Christmas, and Easter clothes could be put in jeopardy.

Grandmother worked in Macy's department store in Manhattan and received a discount on purchases. She determined what we all wore. Her job title was head matron. I always thought she had some type of office job. Eventually, by the time I reached high school, I found out *matron* was just a fancy word for female custodian. So Granny cleaned toilets in Macy's and bought our clothes with her employee discount. She never mentioned she cleaned toilets.

Father's voice was high-pitched when he sang and when he was angry, especially when he had a few too many. He and my older brother once even had a humorous confrontation, like something out of a Martin and Lewis comedy routine.

Father: Why did you wear your new school clothes?
Son: Maybe I'd see someone from my school and I wanted to look good.
Father: You goddamn Gom, who the hell is going to say hello to you anyway!
Son: Don''t know I just wanted...

Before my brother could finish his thought, Dad administered "The Slap" with his good left arm.

The slap always traveled from the ear to the lips. It had a distinct popping sound followed by my brother's yelp.

Mother: Leave the boy alone!
Father: He wore his new clothes here!
Silence.

Dad never slapped me. I had chronic childhood illnesses like sinuses, swollen glands, and the beginnings of asthma. I was off-limits, as were the girls.

My younger brother and Mom received their fair share of smacks, but me, never.

The youngest brother, prone to hysterics, would scream for hours when attacked. He would go into a trance-like state and just howl. He saw one of our dogs get hit by a car once and had to be taken to Dr. Miller's for a shot because he never stopped screaming.

Mother's last slap, had been several years before, the result of dad's drunkenness on one of his weekend visits. He slapped her hard after she called him a drunk and told him he couldn't sleep in the house. She fell to the floor, out cold. Dad wasn't about to sleep in the barn or his car.

My older brother ran off. The girls fell on the floor and tried to wake Mother while the screamer started up. I ran a half mile to the neighbors to call the cops. We had no phone for several years due to our mother's neglect to pay the utility bills.

Neighbors assembled at our house, cops came, and the ambulance siren blared up the road to complete the drama.

Mother lay unconscious at the hand of Father. The state trooper who responded to the call took our father outside and talked with him for a long time. Sergeant Malone returned a few days later to talk to mother. He said her husband faced real jail time if he ever had to come to our house again. As for our neighbors, Dad gave them one more reason to hate us.

After my older brother's slap for the school clothes incident, things returned to normal—normal in the sense that our father kept up his drinking, another round of drinks as we sat and watched.

With few customers in the Blue Moon, no one urged father to play the piano or sing.

Bernie came to explain that since school was going to start the next day, her daughter needed her help to fix her hair special for the first day and so she needed to leave early.

Bernie asked our father if he wouldn't mind going to the bar to get his drinks since George didn't like to wait tables.

George did wait tables, but he refused to wait on ours.

Dad watched Bernie walk to the bar. She took off her apron, spoke briefly to George, and walked towards the door, making sure to attract Dad's attention. Bernie called out his name and waved to him as the door closed behind her.

Once she was out the door, Father began to shift nervously in his seat. He got up and announced he needed to get cigarettes from the car. My brother looked on the table and saw the half-full pack of Chesterfield's.

"But you have smokes here," he called after him.

Definitely a "slap" moment, but Father seemed to be in a hurry.

As soon as he was out the door, Mother asked me to her table.

"Where is he going?" she demanded.

"He said he was out of cigarettes. He went to the car to get some more," I responded.

We sat quietly for about ten minutes waiting for Father's return.

My mother called me over again and asked that I go check on our father.

"That son of a bitch rotten bastard is drunk, and he probably fell on the parking lot or something. Go check on him," our mother commanded.

As the dutiful middle child, I was out the door. I went first to our car and looked to see if he'd had fallen asleep in the back seat. Not there!

I started back into the bar when I heard a familiar sound coming from the pines on the side of the Blue Moon. It was the noise our father made when he slept, a mix between a grunt and a snore. Though our father sang tenor, he definitely grunted and snored as a bass.

I figured Mother's prediction had been correct. He'd had too much to drink and had fallen asleep on the side of the building. Reluctant to approach, I wondered how I should wake him up—shout at him or shake him? I walked toward the sound and smelled smoke. If he was sleeping how in the hell could he be smoking? Maybe he fell asleep with a lit cigarette in his mouth.

As I rounded the corner of the building the sound increased. The grunts and snores turned into animal-like pants. Was Dad having a heart attack? Should I go inside for help? No.

My father was bent over a kerosene barrel, pants down around his ankles as he pumped Bernie underneath him.

She moaned melodramatically as he squeezed her ass. His grunts erupted into squeals. Bernie looked at me, and brought her cigarette to her mouth. She blew the smoke in my direction as Dad pulled himself out of her, bent down, pulled up his pants, and ran a comb through his hair. Didn't even notice me.

I had only seen one other sex act before the 4-H Club's demonstration on cow breeding. The bull had jumped the cow and grunted and snorted, much like my father. The cow, like Bernie, had turned her head to me and looked bored.

I walked backward and retraced my steps until I reached the parking lot. I'd seen an Indian do the same thing in a movie once. The asphalt crunched under my feet as I ran to the front door of the Blue Moon.

What was I going to tell my mother? I just saw our father putting it to Bernie.

I waited in the alcove before I entered the bar. As I walked toward our mother's table, the door swung open behind me. Dad looked drunk and disheveled with his shirt out of his pants and his belt half off.

He never looked at me, but simply announced, "Let's go. Tomorrow is a school day."

My mother never asked me where I found our father or the nature of his prolonged visit to the parking lot.

It would be eight years before I saw my father again. He'd started over, had left us behind. He lived in New York City, remarried, and had another child. Despite his abandonment of our family, he and I spoke occasionally. None of my siblings or my mother ever saw him again after that night at the Blue Moon.

School started the next day. My eighth-grade class consisted of twenty-one students. Tammy sat in the front of the room. I sat in the rear. Throughout the morning, she turned several times to look at me. I pretended I didn't see her. Each time she looked, she had a smile on her face. She waited until noon recess to approach me.

"My mom says you and your bunch was at the Blue Moon last night."

I never answered her; I just nodded my head in the affirmative.

"My mom says that you caught your father fucking her!"

I turned to see if we were surrounded by other classmates. No one was around.

"My mom likes your dad and since he's now gonna be divorced she might want to marry him."

I froze. The thought of having Tammy as a half-sister or step-sister or whatever she would be called frightened me.

"Well, I hope they don't get married," she said, "'cause if they did, we'd never be able to fuck each other."

She stared at me with a blank face.

I smirked at her and walked away.

The Wonder Bar

My name is Terrace Robert Bronson III. People have called me Trey since childhood. The first time I tell folks my full name, they ask if I'm a rich kid.

"No," I say. "As far from rich as one can get."

My attorney asked me to write things down about my life. She gave me a couple yellow legal pads and told me to write.

Born in Jefferson City, Missouri. I still live there today. Locals call it Jeff City. Growing up in Jeff City had its advantages, as well as disadvantages. The state capital offered seemingly everyone a government job. Jeff City's small-town atmosphere, unfortunately, brought with it nosy folks who made other people's business their business.

With a railroad cutting through town, Jeff City boasted a right and wrong side of the tracks. The Bronsons lived on the wrong side of the tracks.

Mom had a job with the state, a janitor at the capitol building. She was well-liked. Sometimes in stores or shops, government official or office workers would say hello to her. She whispered at me to be good so people couldn't say bad things about her at work.

My father never held what would be considered a steady job. He liked to work on cars. He fixed them up, sold them, and made a few dollars here and there. He had an affinity for the booze too. His paycheck usually went toward Falstaff beer or Mound City whiskey.

I kept to myself in high school. In Jefferson City, the school, like the town, was pretty segregated: poor kids, Negro kids, and rich kids. Rich kids kept to themselves, as did the coloreds and the poor. There were plenty of pretty girls, but they usually migrated toward the rich crowd.

I never dated in high school. Instead I ran cross-country for two years. My dad thought I'd be better off working, so I quit the team and joined the workforce.

My senior year of high school my counselor called me into his office. There was a man in uniform. He must have seen that I was scared, and the first thing he said was, "Trey, I want you to meet Sergeant Sam Reed. He's an Air Force recruiter and he wants to talk to you."

Sergeant Sam explained the aptitude test I had taken my junior year. It revealed my exceptionally high score in the area he called "spatial relationships." He went on to say that people with my scores were needed to run radar equipment for the United States Air Force. He asked me if I wanted to discuss it with my parents. At eighteen, soon to graduate, I chose to sign up without their permission. Mom cried. Dad grunted, took a big chug of Mound City, and chased it with a Falstaff.

In July of 1964, I began basic training outside Kansas City, Missouri, at Wright-Whitman Air Base.

I stayed at Wright-Whitman for advanced individual training in radar and special NORAD training.

I figured they'd send me some place like Alaska, Japan, or Europe so I could keep track of communist planes that attempted to sneak into US air space.

I wound up at a small radar tracking station in Queen City, Missouri, about twenty miles outside Kirksville in November of 1965.

The job was easy. I stared at green screens eight hours a day. Never caught one commie plane who dared invade our air space.

An NCO club, where most of the guys hung out after their shifts, was the sole entertainment on base.

After living with my father for nineteen years, the smell and effect of alcohol posed no temptation for me. Mom made sure I attended services at the First Baptist Church every Sunday.

My fellow airmen would get drunk and do it all over again the next day.

Some guys drove to Kirksville to get dates with town girls. College girls were considered off-limits.

As the guys said, "We kinda stuck out like sore thumbs with our short hair and all."

I stayed on base as much as possible. Bored as I was, I wanted to make sure I didn't venture into Kirksville and get into trouble like many of the guys had done.

I wanted to keep my record clean so I could get out of Missouri and go some place exciting. The American troops were being deployed to Vietnam, my next stop after Queen City.

I stayed on base over Thanksgiving and Christmas. I could have gone home but the idea of returning without some impressive stories about my Air Force career wasn't something I relished.

The winter of 1965–66 was brutal in northeast Missouri. Cold and snow set new records.

By February of '66, I'd developed a bad case of cabin fever. I paced the barracks, desparately need something to do.

John Onthank was an airman in our barracks group. A good enough guy, he liked to talk to anyone who'd listen. The other airman played up to him since he had a 1965 Mustang convertible. John let the guys take his car into Kirksville.

"Fill her up with gas, and she's yours," he would say.

Though the guys all talked to John, behind his back they joked about him being some type of queer boy.

He'd sit in the common area of the barracks waiting for a guy to use the showers. John took long showers in the mornings and led discussions about girls in the evenings.

He was sitting in the common area one day when I asked him if I could use his Mustang. Dr. Zhivago was playing at the Kennedy Theater. I asked him if he wanted to join me. He declined my invitation but reminded me to fill the tank.

At the Kennedy Theatre, I settled in and slept through most of the movie. The one thing I did remember about Dr. Zhivago was Julie Christie, the most beautiful woman in the world.

The movie let out about nine-thirty. The guys had said I should go to Pagellia's Pizza on the square. "Best pizza ever," they all claimed.

When I arrived, the place sure did smell good. My waitress, Donna, had long, silky blonde hair like Julie Christie. The resemblance stopped there. Donna sported a large nose and mouthful of big teeth. Mom would've called her horse-faced.

To me, a lonely man, Donna would do. She'd be my Julie Christie for the night. She took my order and called me solider boy. I didn't correct her. We were airmen, not soldiers.

She sat down next to me, and we talked after she served me my pizza.

"I get off at eleven. Do you want to meet me at the Wonder Bar?"

"I'm only twenty."

"Don't matter none. They see you're military and all with that big green parka, they won't ask. Plus, if I'm with you they won't ask me neither," she said.

I told her I had a Mustang. I could pick her up or wait.

"I'll meet you there, solider boy."

The Wonder Bar was a smoky, dirty place, and most of the people at the bar were old and poor. A few men played shuffle board. One guy pissed at the open urinal next to the game table.

I walked to the bar, and the bartender asked what I wanted. I'd always ordered cokes at the NCO. The first thing that popped into my head was Mound City Whiskey and Falstaff. The bartender asked me if I wanted the top-shelf stuff. The patrons at the bar laughed.

"We sell Mound City in half pints only for a buck fifty, and the Falstaff would be another fifty cents"

The bartender placed the beer and whiskey and asked if I wanted a glass.

Before I could answer, an old woman appeared next to me.

"If he don't want a glass! I sure as hell does."

She was disheveled and smelled of cigarettes and beer.

My mother's brother, Jake, used to tell me that poverty had its own smell. He was a residential repairman. He said you could always tell a person's fortunes from the smell of the houses and their personal smells. He claimed poor people never had good plumbing so their homes always stunk like sewage.

This woman at the bar reeked of poverty. A stench of cheap flowery perfume hung in the air around her like a steady ring of flies circling a pile of dog shit in the yard.

"Well, are you gonna open that bottle and share with a lady?"

"Lou, leave the kid alone," said the bartender.

"Sonny, do you want company."

I told her I expected my friend at eleven.

"Well let's have a little drink before your little friend arrives."

The bartender looked at me. I nodded, and he placed a glass in front of her and poured her drink.

"Well here's to you, sonny." She held up her drink, toasted the air, and drained the glass in one swallow.

I picked up the whiskey bottle and filled my mouth and swallowed. The whiskey burned all the way down. I grabbed for the beer and took a big gulp.

The old woman laughed and asked if I drank much.

I took another swallow of whiskey chased with beer.

I'd asked Mom once what whiskey tasted like, and she had likened it to taking a breath of air in hell and beer like cold cat piss.

The old woman reached for the bottle and poured another.

I ordered a second bottle of Mound City and more beers.

Old Lou began to rub my leg. I got hard, and she noticed.

"Sonny, I can make that thing go away for ten dollars. We can step into the alley."

I had never been drunk before. Heck, I'd never had a drink before. A few more minutes and Donna would arrive. A few less drinks, and my life would be different.

We both left the bar. My legs were weak. I steadied myself on the bar stool. She locked my arm and walked me past the shuffle board table to the alley way.

The alley was covered with ice. Lou moved me toward the trash cans. She sat on one can, unzipped my fly, took out her top teeth, and stuck them in her coat pocket for safe keeping.

I don't know if it was the cold February night or divine intervention, but I got soft and pushed the old woman away.

The old woman looked up from her garbage can and began to laugh.

All I saw was her red lips and the dark hole of her mouth.

"What's the matter, sonny boy? You afraid of a little old lady's blow job?"

I zipped my fly, turned, and walked away. She followed me, cursing. I don't even want to repeat what she said her words were so vile.

I wanted to get back to the bar, drink some cokes, and wait for Donna.

The old woman whirled up behind me and hit my back. "You owe me ten bucks, you little prick!"

I turned to her, and she was up in my face. I pushed her away, and she dropped to her butt on the ice.

She began to scream and called me more vile names.

"You must be queer, you rotten son of a bitch. Yes, you are a queer boy!"

On all fours like a dog, she struggled to get up but fell back again.

She began to laugh and screamed, "Yes, I gonna call the law on you, boy. Taking an old lady into the alley and trying to rape her. You'll do time!"

My momma had given me a pair of dress cowboy boots for high school graduation. I wore them when I'd go out. They were black with blunt toes and hand-tooled leather.

I kicked the old woman in the side of her head with my dress boots. Her bottom teeth shot across the icy ground. Finally, she shut up. I must have kicked her about a half dozen more times. Black drops of her blood dotted the dirty alley.

I drove back to base with the windows down. The cold air on my face sobered me up.

I went to my room and waited. I heard the commotion about two hours later. A bunch of people gathered in John Onthank's room. After words were exchanged, they all came to my room.

Town police, sheriff's deputies from Appanoose County, Missouri Highway Patrol, and Air MP's were all at my door.

According to their reports, Donna did show up at the Wonder Bar a little after eleven that night. When questioned, she told the law I was an airman who drove a Mustang. She didn't know my name.

And now I'm back in Jefferson City, in state prison on death row. My lawyer's attempting an appeal—she claims I wasn't read something called my Miranda Rights.

I told her I would write everything down just the way I remembered. I also doodled on the yellow paper. I drew a map of Missouri. I drew a line from Jeff City to Wright-Whitman Airforce Base, then Kirksville, back to Jeff City. It created a large triangle.

So that's the story of my life—an obtuse triangle.

The Red Room

The fall of 1968 should have been better. A senior at Northeast Missouri State University, I expected to graduate in June of '69.

What made fall particularly bad was that the money I earned over the summer, I gave to my mother for a family emergency. A family emergency meant she was broke. It was a state of grace she managed to stay in her entire life.

With only my fall tuition paid, I needed another job to supplement my existence in Kirksville.

Working five nights a week at a local pizza house, I earned about forty dollars a week. I required another forty for basic survival.

That meant another job. My boss at the pizza house recommended I check with the local beer distributor who had a job opening from twelve to five daily and included Saturday mornings. Total income: forty dollars. My financial situation, solved. My dream of a carefree senior year sans full-time work, gone.

I never had an interview with my new boss. I called, and he asked if I possessed a valid driver's license and if I was twenty-one.

He gave me an address and asked me to report to work at one the next afternoon.

The beer warehouse occupied a converted factory off Highway 63. When I entered the brick and tin building, an overpowering stench of stale beer hit me like a Mack truck. I later surmised that the stinky hops permeated my clothes too. My new ritual after work was to immediately shed my smelly clothes, scrub the brewery out of my skin in the shower, and enjoy the freshness in some clean duds.

Jack Dempsey was all of five foot five. He weighed in at close to two hundred pounds. His father had named him after the great Irish boxer.

What he lacked in physical stature, he more than made up for in bullishness. Demps, as he was known, wore a simple uniform: blue pants and light blue shirt adorned with a Schlitz beer logo on the breast pocket. In addition, he kept a White Owl cigar clenched between yellowed teeth on the left side of his mouth that was seldom lit but remained omnipresent even during conversation.

"Hank at the pizza joint told me you was a good kid. Honest too. Look, I'm in a fix today. One of my drivers called in sick and I hafta make delivers." Demps took a breath and continued.

"One of the occupational hazards here, drivers turn into drunks and miss work. Anyways, I gotta get this beer out and you gotta deliver kegs to the Wonder Bar, Tap Room, and the Red Room. Go to the Red Room first. Old John will explain the kegs to you and, fuck, I forgot what I was gonna say. Oh yeah, you can drive a stick shift?"

I nodded my head, but Demps didn't notice.

"The keys are in the pickup. Deliver the kegs, collect the money, come back here, and clean up the warehouse."

Demps turned and walked toward the beer truck.

So much for introductions or tough interview questions like "Where do you see yourself in five years?"

I knew the bars. The Wonder Bar was a townie place college kids stayed away from. The locals tended to be mean and inhospitable to the college crowd. My freshman year, an enlisted man from the Air Force base had taken an old hooker out in the alley and managed to kick her to death. The Tap Room was the bar of choice for the fraternity and social crowd, the Red Room the place to go if you were already drunk or didn't have a good fake ID. The ten-cent draft beers were particularly popular.

Taking Demps's advice, I stopped at the Red Room first.

My eyes took a moment to adjust as I entered.

Despite its name, the Red Room was not red but smoke-covered dirty beige littered with beer signs and old movie posters. I approached the bar and spoke to the barmaid.

"Mr. Dempsey sent me here to deliver—"

I was cut off by a loud "Who the fuck are you talking about?"

Another voice joined in from the end of the bar. "Della Ray, for Christ-sake, leave the kid alone. He's talkin' about Demps. The kid's probably here to deliver beer. Demps told me he was gettin' a new keg boy."

"Well, Mr. Old John, since when have you been in charge of this place, you piece of dog shit?"

I turned from Della Ray and shuffled to the end of the bar. As I neared, my eyes adjusted to the dimness.

"Uhm, John?" I asked.

"Hey kid. Everyone calls me Old John. Demps told me he was hiring a new keg boy and asked if I'd be kind enough to show you the ropes and all."

The voice was refined. Not the type of voice I'd expected to hear in a northeastern Missouri bar.

Old John motioned for me to sit on the bar stool next to him. As I sat down, I noticed Old John's yellowed skin and red eyes, not bloodshot but actually red with a yellow base tint. He extended his hand.

"My name is John McCarthy, but since I've been in Kirksburg here for going on fifteen years everyone refers to me as Old John. It's a moniker I received in college. I consider it a distinction."

Before I had a chance to introduce myself, John proclaimed, in his deep accented voice, "And you, son, forever more will be Beer Boy."

"Demps mentioned I should come here first and you could show me the ropes."

"Excellent, man, that Mr. Jack Dempsey, an excellent man. First things first. Go to your truck and retrieve the keg. I'll walk you through the rest. Hustle now, son, you're cutting into my precious drinkin' time."

I heaved the keg over to the curb and proceded to drag it into the Red Room. The door opened and Old John was there with his arms extended.

"Beer Boy, don't expect anyone to be your doorman. You've got to learn to twirl the leg cart and prop the door open with your ass. I'll give you a pass this time, but don't expect it again."

John stepped out of the bar and onto the sidewalk and held open the door as I bucked the keg over the threshold into the dimness of the bar.

In the brief second I looked at John in the sunlight, I noticed his skin was a definite yellow.

His face was pink and pock-marked. His neck seemed to hang over the collar of his Ban-Lon shirt that was soiled by a variety of foods and sweat stains. He had a thin build with a bloated potbelly right below his chest. This was the one and only day I saw Old John in the sunlight away from his bar stool.

Once in the bar, Old John's voice guided me. "Pull the keg behind the bar, and I'll walk you through the rest."

From his bar stool, Old John's voice was placid, much like a seasoned college professor's reassurance before a big test.

My eyes had not yet readjusted when I walked backward down the bar to the tapers.

Suddenly, Old John yelled out, "Stop, Beer Boy! You got an obstruction on the road."

I eased the keg down onto the slat boards behind the bar and turned my head away from Old John.

Between me and the keg stood Della Ray. "I don't have all fuckin' day for you to stand there with your thumb up your ass. Get that educated moron on the bar stool to help you hook it up and get the hell out of here."

Della Ray was extremely unattractive. Her hair was bright bottle red and done in what can only be described as Shirley Temple frizzy. The pocks in her face were filled with thick pancake makeup, and she had rouged cheeks the size of baseballs. I thought I'd offer her an opportunity to move around me and the kegs, but her girth would have prevented any movement past the cart and keg. Her bar uniform consisted of a white starched shirt, buttons ready to burst, and black pants looked to be painted on, straining at the seams. A red apron rode on the top of her belly.

As she stared at me, she placed her arms on top of her girth.

"Miss, I will—" I offered before she quickly cut me off.

"Don't miss me, you little pissant! Just get this shit out of here so I can get back to work."

As much as Old John's voice sounded foreign, Della Ray's sounded right at home.

"Del, let the man do his job," pleaded Old John.

"Listen, you fuckin' retarded mental case, you do your job and I'll do mine. Get this little fucker outta here before I really close my temper."

With that, Della Ray turned and walked back toward the kitchen.

Della was out of ear range when Old John spoke again. "Don't mind her, Beer Boy. She's the type of woman who puts the capital C in cunt. I'll never know why the hell I ever married her."

"Married?" I couldn't believe my ears.

"You seem shocked," he said with mock amusement in his voice.

"Well, I just thought that..."

"Oh yeah, you just thought that a good-looking guy like myself could do better than to marry Bride-zilla. She out-guns me by twenty years and has close to a hundred pounds on me, too."

I tried to do the math quickly in my head. Old John was about fifty—Della Ray couldn't be in her seventies.

"Beer Boy, stop the mental masturbation. I'm thirty-five and crazy woman is fifty-three."

"Thirty-five?"

"Yeah, and you're wondering why they call me Old John. I know." Old John nodded his head as he read my mind. "I know. We got the rest of the semester to commiserate on my predicament. For now let's get that keg hooked up and get you out of here before the bitch returns."

With his calm voice Old John walked me through the steps to change the keg. "Turn off the gas or you'll have foam shooting over the bar." The word *bar* seemed to have and extra *r* and *h* attached to when he pronounced it.

"Remember to always check the gas and get it at thirty-two PSI. Hit the large wingnut to the left. The keg will hiss as you loosen it—don't be scared. Once loosened, keep turning its wingnut off the top of the keg, then when fully loosened, pull up on the rod and it'll come out of the keg. Always do this while the keg is in the cooler. If you do it outside it could spit beer all over the place. And if you have a barmaid like Della you're really gonna be fucked."

Old John paused to sip his beer. "Now, pull the dead soldier out."

The lightness of the keg without beer amazed me.

"A full keg weighs in at a hundred and fifty-six point five pounds. Respect that, Beer Boy. If you ever have one roll on you, it can cripple. Now pull the rod out and place the empty behind ya."

The rod slipped out. I moved the keg as instructed.

"Now here comes the tricky part. You take the rod, hit it into the keg, and turn the wingnut to the right. Don't hesitate or stop your motion or we'll both be baptized by Milwaukee's Finest."

I placed the rod on the top of the keg and pushed. The steel rod broke and traveled twenty-three inches to the bottom of the keg.

"To the right quickly," Old John offered quietly.

Once secure, I stepped back and waited, anticipating the worst.

"Now push the big boy into his new home. Turn the gas to thirty-two and get a pitcher off the bar. Get yourself a glass."

I turned and retrieved the pitcher and glass.

"Now pull the taper towards you. It's going to spit and sputter, but no harm done. Keep it pulled back until the beer runs clear."

The taper made a hiss, and a gurgle sound produced white foam. Within five seconds the clean amber of the freshly-tapped keg appeared. I took the half-filled pitcher and turned toward the bar sink.

"Whoa, Beer Boy. We never waste beer here. You know people in Arab countries are sober. I get the dregs, always. Now grab that glass and pull yourself a drink. Kinda have a celebration."

I drew my glass from my virgin keg, and Old John said, "Let's toast to your first keg."

Della Ray's voice shattered the calm moment. "Make sure you leave thirty-five cents on the bar. There's no free lunches here."

"For God sakes, Del, it's the kid's first tapped keg."

"I don't care if it's his mother's funeral, everyone pays here, everyone."

Old John and I quickly touched glasses.

"May your life be long and full of adventures," he said in a meloncholy voice.

"When you two queers are done fucking each other, let me know so I can have your new boyfriend write the check."

Della Ray threw a blank check on the counter and walked back to the kitchen.

Old John cleared his throat. "Beer Boy, fill out the check. Write in thirty-two dollars and make it out for today's date, pay to the order of Kirksville Distributors."

As I filled in the check, Old John said, "I know you may find it difficult to believe in this day and age, but my dear wife never learned how to read or write. I tried to teach her, but to no avail. I believe she has a condition known as Johnson Syndrome. It's a malady for people who have the intelligence to read and write but refuse to do so. It's often referred to as 'reading refusal.' Yes, my lovely wife is definitely a victim of the Johnson Syndrome."

Old John must have picked up on the puzzled look on my face because before I could speak, he said, "Patience, my son. We have many more days of social intercourse ahead of us." Old John asked me about my next stops and gave me some friendly advice on how to handle the various personalities of the bar personnel I would have to deal with.

At the warehouse the next day, I told Demps about my run-in with Della Ray and my conversation with Old John.

"Tell you what, give that fat cunt all the room she needs. As far as Old John goes, the man is the salt of the earth. I mean, you don't find people better then John. Nor do you find anyone worse than that bitch of a wife of his. She is only a goddamn barmaid and she struts around like she is the Queen of Seba."

I asked Demps to explain "the how" of them as a couple.

Demps said, "I don't gossip or try to share in people's personal business. But I tell you, a daily visit with Old John should give you a PhD in life philosophy, at the least."

I didn't pressure Demps for further explanation.

The Red Room went through a keg a night, not a large amount for a college bar but enough to keep the doors open and the likes of Della Ray and Old John employed.

A keg a day also meant daily afternoon visits from me, the Schlitz Beer Boy.

"Beer Boy, are the Cardinals going to win again this year?" Old John asked, as I maneuvered myself behind the bar.

"Don't ask me. I'm not really a baseball fan. I still haven't forgiven the Dodgers for leavin' Brooklyn."

"So you're a Dodgers fan, are ya?"

"Not anymore."

Old John's laugh was interrupted by a low rumbling cough from deep inside his chest. He took a large gulp of his draft beer, closed his eyes, pursed his lips, and attempted to talk again.

"So what's a nice Midwest boy like you grieved over a bunch of East Coast misfits like the Brooklyn Dodgers?"

"Former East Coast misfit," I shot back. Before Old John could respond I added, "The Dodgers and I both have a lot in common—we both left the East Coast. They made it to California, and I only made it to Iowa and now Missouri."

"So you're a Yankee are ya. I thought you had some redeeming character about you."

I explained to Old John that I'd grown up in New York, both down state on Long Island and upstate in the Catskills. My parents divorced, and I wound up living in Iowa after my mother remarried. Two years in Iowa to finish high school, now in Kirksville to finish college.

"So you've been traveling the country, I see. Ever been to Boston?"

I hesitated before I answered. "We lived in Boston for about six months. My mother met this guy, she packed us up, we took off for Boston. Things didn't work out so we wound up in Iowa."

"How'd ya like Boston?"

"Great, except for the accents. It took me six months to figure out what they were saying, then we moved."

"Talked kinda funny did they now?" Old John's voice had a mocking amusement to it.

"Well, if you're fifteen years old a new place is going to have its set of oddities."

"Speaking of oddities, what do you think of Denny McClan? People say he's going to win the series for Detroit. Any feelings on that?"

"Like I said, I don't follow baseball, but if you want to talk about politics I am up to speed on that."

"So who's gonna win in the fall? Nixon, Humphrey, or Wallace?"

"I'm pulling for Humphrey. Nixon and Wallace are both nut jobs," I said.

"What makes you pull for the Democrat?"

"I think Nixon will get us further into Vietnam."

"You think the war is bad?"

"Yes!"

"Tomorrow I want you to deliver us last so we can have a little talk about politics, war, and the overall state of our precious world."

"No problem," I said.

The next day I asked Demps if I could alter the route to deliver to the Red Room last.

I explained that Old John wanted a few minutes to talk, and I just wanted to let him know.

"First of all, kid, there are no good ways to do a keg route. The reason I started you at the Red Room first was to have Old John run you through the routine. You can do your route any way you want. I pay you for four hours a day. If you do your job in three who's to know."

"Thanks, but being new on the job, I wanted to go through the boss first."

"Good thinking, kid, but tell me, whatta you think of Old John?"

"I really don't know. He seems like an intelligent guy. But then I look at his wife and wonder how smart can he be?"

Demps's laugh made me pause.

"Good observation."

"I guess my answer would be I don't know."

"Like I said, kid, just listen to him and stay away from that nasty wife of his."

I entered the Red Room and immediately heard the voice from behind the bar.

"We don't need your fuckin' kegs today," Della Ray said.

I lowered the keg to the bar floor and searched for Old John.

"Your boyfriend is in the back cleanin' up the shitters. Maybe you should go back there and suck each other off."

I moved the keg toward the pool table out of the customers' way.

I settled on a bar stool two down from Old John's perch. Clearing my throat I spoke to Della. "Give me a draft and pour one for John."

"You got ID?"

At first I thought she was joking until she walked directly in front of me. "ID or no beer."

I reached for my wallet and showed her my driver's license.

She took her reading glasses from her bar apron and examined the license front and back.

She threw the license back across the bar as Old John parked himself two seats down.

"Why the fuck are you cardin' him, Ray? He delivers our beer. He's got to be at least twenty-one."

"Hey, genius, stick to cleanin' the shitters, and I'll run the bar. Crazy bastard."

I sipped my beer and meekly said, "I'm buyin' for John too."

"No you're not—he's had enough," she said and lumbered off to the kitchen.

"Sorry about the ID thing. We got busted again last night about five and the cops shut us down. Some little sorority girl had her big sister's ID. The cops came in to check everyone and the face on the license didn't match hers, so they closed us down for the night." He rose from his stool with his seven-ounce glass in his hand, flipped the Schlitz tape with his right, and five seconds later he had a perfect glass of beer with a half-inch head. He quickly retreated to his bar stool, a satisfied grin on his face.

"Great pour," I said.

"Years of practice. Can't waste a drop. You know people in India are sober?"

He chuckled at his own joke.

"I guess you won't need a keg."

"You got it in here, so just take it to the walk-in cooler and remind Demps that we were closed down. Tell Demps he has friends at liquor control in Jeff City and he'll make sure we don't get too many days closed."

I delivered the keg to the cooler and returned to my seat.

"Looks like the Cards and Detroit will be at it again this year. Games start this week in Detroit. Oh yeah, you're the guy who's still thinking the Dodgers should come back to Brooklyn."

"No love for baseball here. I'm more a fan of politics, remember?"

John paused before answering. "I usually don't forget stuff, but lately the old mind is not so quick. I remember, politics. You want Humpty Dumpty Humphrey to win, right?"

"Better than Wallace or Nixon," I said.

"Nixon will win, Beer Boy. Americans like the lies he tells better than the others. Wallace, he's too crazy, but he'll get his share of votes."

"So you think Nixon will win?"

"Oh yeah, those Republican always got something up their sleeves. Just like Eisenhower, telling people he would go to Korea and stop the war. Well he did but he never stopped the war."

"I thought the Korean Conflict was settled by a cease-fire."

"Korean Conflict!" shouted Old John. "Is that what the fuckers are still calling it?"

Old John moved forward on his stool to make sure his shout didn't get Della Ray out of the kitchen.

He gulped his beer and reached over the bar for a refill. This time I caught a strong whiff of stale urine coming from his body.

His hands trembled as he skunked his second beer. His hands shook enough to cause him to spill some of the beer into the drain. He pulled the glass back to the bar and made a quick sign of the cross. "God forgive me for wasting this precious liquid of life." A smiled spread across the old man's face.

"You Catholic?" I asked.

"Of course I'm Catholic. And you?"

"Yes."

"Sorry I shouted about that Korean Conflict thing, just a bone of contention for me being a veteran and all." With that said, Old John raised his glass and sucked down his beer.

"You were in the Second World War?" I asked.

"No, Beer Boy, I was in the Korean War. I was fifteen when World War Two ended. God damn, I told you I was thirty-five."

Della Ray came from the kitchen.

"I told the kid to put the beer in the cooler," John told her matter of factly.

"Well, genius, you can tell your little boyfriend that we don't need no beer, so he can take it back. Cause I ain't paying him."

With that said, Della Ray retreated back to the kitchen.

"Sorry about the keg thing, Beer Boy. That old bitch is the boss, and if you don't take it she'll cause hell with your boss, Demps. She'll tell him the Red Room will go to Bud on tap."

"No problem. I'll put to the keg back on the truck and see you tomorrow."

"Look, Beer Boy, I still owe you a conversation about politics. Del does her banking about one. Can you juggle your route to be here then?"

"Look forward to it."

The next day, I pulled the keg into the Red Room and noticed four fraternity boys playing pool, Old John standing behind the bar. He motioned me to come closer.

"Just in time, Beer Boy." His voice was low and strained.

"Big favor, Beer Boy. I am really not feeling all that good—could you spot me behind the bar until Del gets back?"

Old John made his way down to the end of the bar. His left hand held the edge of the bar and stool to stool for support.

He finally settled into his seat with a loud sigh.

"Are you sick or something?" I asked.

"Is the fucking pope a little Catholic?"

"Have you been to the doctor or what?"

"Beer Boy, they can't cure what I got, and what I got is death coming on. Probably quicker then I or the fucking doctors thought."

"What—" was all I was able to get out before Old John shot back.

"I got cirrhosis of the liver, Beer Boy. Fifteen straight years of living on beer, bar food, and Camels have done me in. Yeah, I had to give up the Camels. I was coughing so hard I could hardly keep my match lit."

Old John laughed. "Yeah, the doctors told me years ago to cut back on the booze, but what the hey? I love my beer. Now I pay the piper or whoever is going to collect my wretched body."

Old John was interrupted by the banging of a pool cue against the side of the table, the Red Room's sign for another round or pitcher of beer.

Old John spoke said quietly, "Would you mind pouring a pitcher for those fraternity fucks? Collect a buck and a quarter."

I poured the pitcher and walked it to the table next to the pool table.

"Buck and a quarter, boys."

They continued to play, ignoring my request.

Each of them had on blue sweat shirts with yellow letters spelling SIG TAU.

"Gentlemen, a dollar twenty-five please."

The shortest one in the group reached into his pocket and placed five quarters on the table.

He turned to me and said, "Never call a Sig Tau 'boy.'" The others chuckled and returned to their game.

I had seen all of them on campus. Two I had in some of my classes. One on one they were friendly enough, but in packs they tended to get mean.

I returned to the bar, and Old John said, "Listen, don't let them fraternity fucks get to you. They'll be teaching PE in some lonely Missouri town in a few years. The girls they marry will get fat and their kids'll get ugly. These will be the best years of their miserable fucking lives."

Again Old John laughed followed by a low rumble of a cough. "Beer Boy, this is an exceptional special favor, one which I will carry eternally to my grave. I have to check and clean the restroom once a day to make sure the toilet is flushed and take the things hanging down on the wall and use them to pull the rubber screen from the urinal. Would you pull the screen and flush the cigarette butts down the drain? I hate to ask but, I'm not with it today and—"

"Not a problem," I said.

"I promise when you get back, I'll tell you about Korea, politics, and the enviable domination of communism in the world. Just fucking with you about the last part, honest."

Back from the restroom Old John had fresh beer poured for himself and one for me.

"First, before we try to solve the world's problems, I want your take on today's series game in Detroit. Which do you take, the Cardinals or the Tigers? I mean this is important shit, Beer Boy. The balance of the free world is depending on the outcome."

"Cardinals. I take the Cardinals."

"Good selection. I think I'll take Detroit."

"Let me tell you something about the Korean War, Beer Boy." Old John took a long drink and placed his glass on the bar, empty. Old John began his story.

"I was a sophomore at Boston College. It was in the late spring of nineteen fifty when the commies in Northern Korea invaded South Korea. I mean, you got to understand the times. It was the height of the Cold War. Five years after the Second World War and now the commies were in full swing in Korea. All the college boys my age and up with older brothers, uncles, fathers, and whoever telling their tales about how they kicked Jap or Nazi asses. Here we were with a chance to kick ass, big time. I mean, old man Stalin had us all shitting our pants. So out of strict patriotic duty and a few too many beers, a bunch of us signed up for the army.

"Fortunately for some boys, their parents had some clout and got their enlistments reversed. I was too embarrassed to tell my parents that I'd signed up when I was drunk.

"I found myself in basic training in Fort Leonard Wood. I mean right here in the great state of Missouri. Guess I could lie and tell you I was with a great bunch of guys and we were going to be buddies for life. Far from friends, my basic training mates where a harsh collection of riffraffs the draft managed to bring together. I was one of only a few college boys in our training group. The rest of them were street kids, farm boys, and knuckleheads who had the choice of service or jail.

"A lot of our time in basic was spent learning about the evils of communism. We found out the commies don't believe in God and if they ever took over, the first thing they would do would do was burn the churches and kill the priests, nuns, and ministers. Secretly, I was rooting for the commies and thought about a Catholic school and a bunch of nuns I hoped they'd start with first."

Old John paused and looked hard at himself in the bar mirror. A smile crossed his face.

"You know I really don't harbor any hate towards the nuns of St. Agnes. They are a different story that really deserves to be told, but another time. Anyway, back to the commies and the armpit of the world known as Korea.

"Our uncles, brothers, fathers, and cousins had the privilege to go to wars by boat. Six to eight weeks to know the guys you were going to fight and maybe die with. We were airlifted to Korea because the United Nations had called for immediate police action. Since the police needed to be there immediately, the boats were out and the planes were in. Not a great deal of time to forge friendships and all.

"Well, anyhow, here we are a bunch of green recruits with a smattering of World War Two vets heading for Korea to stop the Mongol horde form the north.

I wish I was able to preface my story with great things to come and heroic battles and body counts of commies, but all that never happened for me or my 'buddies.'

"We landed in Korea in November of 1950. You have to remember this was international police action. I think the youth of today would call it a cluster fuck.

"I won't bore you with army talk or battalion armory platoon or whatever crap they now call it.

"We were attached to a Turkish army battalion for supply support. I mean before this the only thing I ever knew of about Turkey is that you eat one every Thanksgiving."

Old John studied his glass, seeming preoccupied. "No humor lost on the youth of today. Let me go on." He sipped his beer.

"Okay, where was I? Oh, yeah, the Turks. Remember, this was a police action. No one really knew what the hell was going on. So when the Turks met up with some people with slanted eyes and yellow skin they began shooting. It was a massacre by the Turks, hundreds of yellow-skinned people where dead.

"Someone figured out that the soldiers killed were South Koreans and not the commie North Koreans.

"Needless to say, panic was the order of the day. By radio, we were ordered to get the hell out of the area lest the Americans be blamed.

"Long story short, we scuttled. The first troops we ran into were the commie North Koreans. So my first day of war, I was captured and wound up a freaking POW."

Old John looked out the back bar window. He swallowed his beer, reached over the counter to draw another, carefully surveying the kitchen area for Della Ray as he did so.

"So here we are surrounded by a bunch of crazy chinks yelling orders at us in Korean. It could have been Martians, for Christ sake. We realized quickly they had no idea what the heck to do with us. I mean in war, things are messy.

"No communications with their commanders, they decided the best thing to do was to march us north over the Yalu River. Once we were in our camp, we would learn through a translator that the Turks actually began to shoot up the South Koreans, killing a bunch of them.

"The translator tried to convince us that the North Korean army had really rescued us from slaughter by our own allies."

"So what happened in camp?" I asked with anticipation.

"Not really much, kid. I mean we weren't tortured or anything—subjected to interrogations, yes, but not really bad stuff."

"How come we read about brainwashing and all that?" I asked.

"Look, kid, we were a bunch of numb-nut kids, the oldest being some twenty-two years old from Oklahoma. They realized we were not high priority. Was there torture? The answer is simply yes. But for our group, no."

Old John drank the rest of his draft and stared at the empty glass in front of him.

"How did you guys pass the time?"

"Glad you asked. The fun part was the re-education classes they put us through. I mean, they had a simple curriculum that was basic Marx-Lenin, communism—good. Capitalism—bad. We were in classes without a translator for a while until they realized they had a real college boy in their ranks, me. Once they realized I had college they turned the classes over to me."

"They let you teach the classes?"

"Keep it down. You're gonna disturb the other customers." John turned and in dramatic voice, announced to an empty bar, "I'm sorry my young friend is so excited about my time in a Korean POW camp."

I was about to apologize when Old John waved his hand. "Kid, please understand when people are fuckin' with you, please!"

Old John smiled and reached for another draft of Schlitz.

"Anyway, the teaching about Marx-Lenin and communism turned out to be the highlight of our days. I mean, with me as the teacher I turned Marx into the Marx Brothers.

"Our translator was replaced by a low-level enlisted man. I was given a script, and I read it to our men. But as soon as the guy who couldn't understand a lick of English fell asleep, the comedy routine began. Sometimes we got so rowdy we woke the little chink with our laughter. He'd jump up and then sit down and resume his sleep.

"You can't imagine the acts of sodomy that Karl Marx and Vladimir Lenin committed as illustrated by my crude cartoons."

"So I guess it wasn't hard for you?" I asked.

"Have you philosophy teachers ever tried to explain the concept of heaven and hell? For some of my American comrades the prison life was extremely difficult. No contact with the outside world, not anything. Some of them snapped, committed suicide. Others ratted me out and the classes stopped along with the extra rations.

"By the time we were released in August of 1953 you had groups of very dysfunctional and very crazy American soldiers."

"So what happened when you were released?" I asked.

Old John once again looked into the mirror and stared hard before he began again.

"At first, we were treated as heroes, then some of the guys mentioned the games we played during the 'classes' and some of the higher-ups got wind and they tried to put an 'aiding the enemy' on me with a couple of other guys. There was the threat of a court-martial and all that other crap. They wanted us to sign releases stating that we were tortured, I refused. One guy, thinking he would be labeled a communist or a traitor, actually killed himself. They sent us back to the states and ran us through the final debriefings at Fort Leonard Wood.

"After all the army's shit, the only thing I wanted to do was to get back to school quickly. It was October 1953, Kirksville State Teachers College was on the quarter system at the time, and I enrolled a few days after leaving

Fort Leonard Wood. And that is what I have done and been here in heaven ever since and have not left."

"You mean you never left Kirksville?" I asked.

"Never. Got as far as La Plata a couple of times but never got on the train. Yes siree, stuck right here in K'Ville, MO, and proud of it."

"I've gotta go. See you tomorrow with a keg." I said.

Old John waved and returned to his reflection in the bar mirror.

Next day, the Red Room was blocked off by police cars. My first thought—someone had robbed the place. Or worse—something happened to Old John.

I double-parked the truck next to a state highway patrol car. Inside, the city cop and the sheriff's deputy were seated at the bar. The highway patrolman was talking with the owner, Bob Circle. Del stood between them.

I looked down the bar. Old John wasn't there. I looked toward the restroom.

Del turned away when I looked at her. Bob Circle approached me.

"You the new beer boy Old John talked about?"

"Yes."

"We're sorry to break the news, but Old John died about an hour ago. Seems that liver of his finally gave out."

Bob turned from me, addressing Del. "Del, I want you to get home and take care of stuff for Old John."

Del stared at me before she answered Bob. "Bobby, I think I'll stay. I need the money." A wicked smile crossed here face as she kept her gaze my way.

Irish Angels

Patrick attempted to explain why he had to return to the Hamptons for the weekend.

Lilya wouldn't cooperate. "I have bad feelings about you leaving," she said. "I think maybe I never see you again."

Patrick tried to time the evening to a series of events. He made reservations at Tony's, St. Louis's only five-star restaurant. The atmosphere, top notch. The food, divine. The topic of discussion, Patrick's departure to visit family and ease Lilya's fears.

"What makes you think we'll never see each other again?"

"You never understand Russian people. We go by emotions. You go back home and see children and wife and you forget your Russian girlfriend. I become only the 'summer thing' for you."

"By the way that's, 'summer fling' not 'summer thing.'"

"Why you make fun of my English all the time?"

"I am not making fun of your English. I am trying to make a joke!"

"It not funny, way I feel. I feel like I never see you again and you make jokes!" Lilya pouted.

"Hey, we've talked about this before. Irish people tend to make humor out of dark situations. I'm going home for family business reasons. I will be back in a few days. We'll both fly to New York. I promise you the best few days of your life."

Lilya's eyes filled with tears. She knew New York would be the "last few days" she would spend with Patrick. Then what? Back to medicine in Russia? A hundred American dollars a month, if she's lucky. Shitty apartment. No chance for a life.and that was it. She knew once she was back in Moscow, there would be no chance for success. Success as she saw American doctors have success.

The waiter took their order. Patrick knew better than to let Lilya order her own food. Waiters, he felt, had a mean streak in them. They loved to play with pretty young women with foreign accents. At first, Patrick wanted Lilya to struggle through when she ordered. He felt he did her a favor—she was learning English after all. Just another opportunity to use it. But he found it often ruined an evening. Patrick quickly order for both and then returned to the conversation.

"Look, I have to go back East. You'll be fine until I get back."

"What about New York?"

"What do you mean, 'What about New York?' I told you, we'll have a great time," Patrick pleaded.

"I don't care about 'great time.' I want to know what happens to us after New York."

Patrick had no answer. He told Lilya he loved her. Now, "What about New York" meant he'd have to explain, make plans for the future.

"Lilya, what do you want to happen after New York?"

"What you mean, 'What I want?' I have no power here. I am simple Russian doctor who visits your country. I fall in love with man and he asks me what I want. I want you, and I want us to be together, forever. Does that make you understand 'What I want?'"

Patrick fell back into silence. He looked at the table setting, wishing the waiter would bring their drinks and food so he could keep his mouth busy. He knew where this conversation was headed.

"I don't know want to say. I've told you I love you. I've told you I am happy with you." Patrick's voice started to break.

Lilya cut him off before he continued. "If that all true, then you can marry me. Marry me and everything is okay. You will have wife that loves you and son who will love you—what else you want?"

Patrick knew he had to tread carefully. He loved Lilya. The thought of her going back to Russia drove him crazy. Married with children, in name only, the question he dared not answer: would he let this woman get away?

"Lilya, I do love you. I want you to stay in America. I want to marry you. I want us to be a family. Me, you, and your son."

Lilya's hand slid across the table and grasped his. "Thank you so much. You make me happy, and I love you so much." Lilya smiled into Patrick's eyes as she spoke.

Timing was everything. Patrick would rerun this moment over and over in his head; the dreaded video of the situation would haunt him. "As soon as I get back from New York, we'll do some serious planning."

As Patrick spoke these words, Lilya's hand shot from his and retreated under the table. He looked at her, the cold look in her eyes actually frightening him. "What is it?" he asked.

"I want to go home—now!"

"No problem. We can order something in."

"No, I want to go home to my dormitory room."

Lilya had stayed with Patrick for the past three weeks. She occasionally went to her dorm room to check for mail or nap between classes.

"Look, I thought you would understand. I have business and family business to attend to back East so I guess I don't know what the problem is."

"There no problem," she replied coldly.

Lilya stood up and made her way to the entrance. The maître d' rushed to Patrick, spoke to him quietly, and assured him there was no problem. The lady had suddenly taken ill. He discretely handed the man a fifty dollar bill and left after her.

He spotted a woman pacing the sidewalk with a long cigarette in her hand. Every few feet she took a drag, exhaling smoke. Patrick watched for several seconds. At first, thrown off by the cigarette, he didn't think the woman was Lilya.

"I never realized you smoked."

"There are many things you do not realize about me," Lilya said.

"I'll take you home. We can talk or, if you'd like, when I get back from New York."

Lilya threw the cigarette into the street and looked toward Busch Stadium.

Patrick spoke again, struggling to keep up beside her as she walked away quickly.

"You realize I've never taken you to a baseball game."

"Like most things American, baseball is stupid."

"Old saying goes that you will never understand Americans unless you understand baseball."

Lilya led the way across Broadway to Patrick's car.

She continued her fast clip, Patrick practically jogging to keep up. He acquiessed to his taxed lungs and slowed down to catch his breath. So much for youth!

Lilya waited at the passenger door. Patrick usually opened her door but opted for the remote, clicked the unlock button, and announced, "It's open."

The young doctor slid into the Buick, buckeled her seatbelt, crossed her left leg over right, hugged the door, and fixed her eyes out the window. The incident reminded Patrick of the first time he'd given Lilya a ride home to her dorm at Washington University.

How much do you really get to know someone in three weeks?

Without a doubt, the sex—euphoric—the company—rapturous. Patrick loved this woman, but her jealous fury burned against his family. Lilya definitely fit the catagory of controlling girlfriend. Patrick avoided discussion with her for the remainder of the night. He'd call her in the morning, see if she'd cooled off. Maybe wait until Monday when he returned from the Hamptons. Hopefully then they'd make plans for Lilya to stay in America, for her son to join them from Moscow. Plans for a new life.

Patrick would attempt to explain how marriages in America, especially when they involved a lot of money, took time to dissolve. Nice word, *dissolve*. Like something caught in a clogged drainpipe. He needed time to see his children, talk to his wife, seek advice from his father-in-law. Despite the situation with his dead mother-in-law and his wife and kids, Patrick stayed close to his father-in-law, Jack Dausen. They were both Irish. Both shared dark secrets being married to Whitt heirs.

Patrick pulled into the parking lot behind Lilya's dorm. Before the Buick came to a complete stop, Lilya blazed out and up the steps to her dorm.

Good night honey, I love you! he mockingly said to himself.

Patrick drove back to his apartment in the Chase Park Plaza. His thoughts shifted from Lilya to what waited for him in the Hamptons.

A six-thirty flight in the morning meant no sleep for him. The limo driver stood at the end of the exit ramp outside Terminal D at La Guardia. He held a hand-printed card that read Patrick O'Connor. Patrick knew from past experience that everyone wanted to put an O before his name, especially foreigners. In this case, he purposely chose a foreign-run company.

When he'd looked up car services in New York City, a Russian-owned company caught his eye. The outfit called itself White Nights Limo. Patrick called. Got a groggy man with a thick Russian accent on the line, either drunk or sleepy. Patrick hoped the man on the other end wouldn't be his driver. The dopey Russian told Patrick the trip to the Hamptons would cost $350, plus tolls and tip.

Patrick introduced himself to the young Russian limo driver. "Good morning. I'm Patrick Connor. I believe you'll be taking me to the Hamptons."

The driver quickly smiled and grabbed Patrick's carry-on bags.

"Good morning, Mr. O'Connor. Happy to be of service. My name is Dmetri, and I am driver this morning."

Friendly, Dmetri smiled at Patrick and gestured an invitation to the car. With his mild Russian accent, he said, "Please follow me. We will get you home to Hamptons very fast."

Patrick trailed the young man to the lower lobby of the airport past the baggage claims.

"You have more bags maybe?"

Patrick mouthed a no. The driver moved toward the exit.

Patrick liked LaGuardia. It was old, simple, and very predictable. A poor cousin compared to JFK or Newark, but close to the city and without miles of airport to walk through. Patrons new to the airport probably thought it looked like a third-world way station. "It's functional and it's New York," was Patrick's usual reply.

The driver led Patrick through the parking garage to his limo. The limo, a new Lincoln Town car, was very black and very shiny. He opened the door quickly, offering Patrick the backseat. The new-leather smell was intoxicating. It was either a really new car or the driver was one of those idiots who like to use "new car scent" as deodorant. Skillfully, Dmetri manuevered them in and out of morning traffic, onto the 495, headed to eastern Long Island.

Once out of the city, the young man started conversation. "You come to New York very much?"

Patrick explained he really lived in Washington, he had been in St. Louis and had a house on Long Island with his family. He wondered if Dmetri understood. The young man nodded in agreement, laughing at Patrick's hectic lifestyle.

The conversation moved on. The young man explained he'd lived in New York for a few years. A university graduate from St. Petersburg, he studied English while in school. All young Russian people study English. They hoped to come to America. His uncle owned the limo service—he came as a relative on a permanent visa since his mother's emigration in the late eighties.

Presently, Dmetri was studying for his engineering license exam. With a professional engineering license (PE), he'd get a real job as a civil engineer. Dmitri continued to talk about his future, maybe even marriage when the time was right. He praised Russian women and asked Patrick if he knew any Russian women.

At first, Patrick refused to answer. Patrick had learned one thing well from his Russian woman friend:, "Be aware of people who ask too many personal questions."

Patrick's mind rested on his young Russian doctor. Perhaps Dmetri could offer him some insight on the mechanics of the female Russian mind.

"Funny you should ask. I did meet a Russian lady in St. Louis and we have become close over the last month."

The young Russian interrupted Patrick with a loud laugh. "Was she, as we call in Russian, your interpreter or as you may call her, your female lover?"

Patrick hesitated a little before he answered, "Yes, I guess."

Patrick sounded timid, never comfortable when discussions turned to sex. The last month had taught him a thing or two about sex, probably loosened him up a little, but he knew he couldn't open up about his sex life with a stranger.

"We have saying. 'Once you go Russian you never go back.'"

"I thought that was, 'Once you go black you never go back.'"

"Not anymore since so many Russian woman come to New York and the US. Many Americans seek them out for sex and fun. Even cherney men—excuse me—black men seek out Russian woman because they're so good. Few

Russian women like black men. We don't like to see our people with black men."

Patrick felt uncomfortable with the direction of the conversation, so tried to change it.

"My friend was—or is—a doctor. She is in the States to learn American business practices to take home to Moscow. I guess the Russians want to know the pleasures of dealing with HMO's and the wonders of other health insurance carriers."

"Russian doctors are very good," said Dmetri. "Are some of the best in the world. We just not have the money for medicine like Americans."

Dmetri continued after Patrick failed to respond to his comments. "Chinese doctors are also very good doctors. Like Russian doctors, they know that not all medicines come out of pill jar. Natural remedies and the human mind are part of cures. I read last week in New York Times that your government closed down Chinese clinic in Brooklyn because they did not have American doctors. They claim clinic was run by Chinese organized crime. Americans want no competition with their doctors."

Talk of a clinic caught Patrick's attention. Interesting that organized crime would hit on medicine, but why not? Medicine was big business, and crime goes where the money is.

"What about the Chinese clinic in Brooklyn? Sounds like a novel idea," said Patrick.

"What novel idea? Americans think that theirs is the only medicine. People coming to this country trust their own doctors. The Chinese were doing what everyone else does. But, they get caught. Government says that it is criminal, the Chinese organized crime involved. It all a bunch of shit, bunch of real bullshit by government."

Patrick realized Dmetri was agitated by the conversation about the American government, how they treated medical practices outside their own. He had some experience with

Russian doctors, at least on a personal level. He decided to push the envelope a little with Dmetri, see what might be in the future for Lilya if she were to stay in the United States.

"What about Russian doctors in the US? How do they get by?"

Patrick stared at the back of Dmetri's head, waiting for a response. Dmetri looked up into the rearview mirror and stared at Patrick before he responded.

"Russian people like to take care of each other. We have our own means."

"What you're saying is the Russians in New York use Russian doctors that may not be board-certified by the US government."

Patrick gritted his teeth, realizing he'd come off a bit patronizing.

"There are Russian doctors who have graduated from Russian medical schools. Our universities are some of the best in world. It takes up to five years for Russian doctors to pass your American test for certification. Five years of studying and testing and then they must do their residency in US hospitals. We talk now about eight years of a person's life. Why? Because the US government thinks they are better than anyone."

Patrick again sensed the driver's agitation.

Dmetri continued. "I have friend who is Russian doctor. He come here and need to take three American tests before he can be doctor. He works in hospital as an orderly at night and studies all day. Can you imagine doctor made to be orderly in hospital? He works with blacks and Puerto Ricans who don't give shit about patients. He is good doctor. He must play American game to get ahead."

Patrick had one more question before he knew he had to change the subject. After all, the car ride was far from over, and Patrick needed to make nice with Dmetri.

"Dmetri, you mentioned the Times article saying there were elements of Chinese organized crime involved with the clinic in Brooklyn. What about the Russian Mafia—have they gotten into medicine in New York?"

Patrick waited for a response.

Dmetri drove in silence for a few moments before he said, "There is no such thing as Russian Mafia. American government wants to make sure foreigners don't get ahead, so they call good business people mafia. Your newspapers and your shitty book writers like to talk about so-called Russian Mafia. There is no Russian Mafia, only jealous Americans who, despite what they call free markets, cannot keep up with good competition. Please, no more question. I must study road."

Patrick sat back.

Must have touched a small nerve there, hunh, Dmetri?

He'd read articles on the so-called Russian Mafia like everyone else. They'd taken over most of the prostitution and strip joints up and down the East Coast. They smuggled in girls to work massage parlors and gentlemen's clubs. Russians also thrived in the drug trade, cornered the market on ecstasy, offered protection, and supplied New York with the lion's share of loan sharks.

So why not medicine? The Chinese were into it. Why not the Russians? The Lincoln came up on the River Head Exit. Another hour if the Montauk Highway wasn't too backed up.

Patrick loved Long Island. He hated visits home, but he loved the island for its many charms and The Hamptons, overdeveloped with too much money and not enough land. Each trip, Patrick noted the number of old farms turned into villas or condos. Charming nonetheless.

His father-in-law had given him advice about ten years . He'd told him to buy into Montauk Manor. Patrick bought the condo with arrangements to lease it back to management for weekenders and summer vacationers. The condo proved to be a good investment. In addition, it gave him a hideout when things got too hot at the family home in East Hampton.

Patrick awoke from a brief nap. They entered South Hampton. Another half hour to go. Ready to nod off again, he shouted instead. "Stop!"

To their left was a car rental place. Not just any car rental, but the classic cars they rented were the envy of the Hamptons. Parked out front was a beautiful blue '66 Jaguar XKE convertible. Each time Patrick came to the Hamptons, he passed that car and swore the next time he would rent it. Today, he decided, was the day.

"What you mean 'stop?' We are not at Montauk Manor." The driver's voice had an authoritative tone that annoyed Patrick.

"Hey, look, Ivan, I told you to stop, so stop the car, turn it around, and go back to the classic car rental place and we'll all be happy!"

"My name is Dmetri not Ivan, and you pay me to take to Montauk and we are not there. You do not pay for sightseeing trip."

"Look, Dmetri. Let's talk in plain English. Turn this fucking car around now or I'm not going to pay you a red cent, I swear to God. I'll call and cancel my credit card to your company."

The driver hit the brakes hard. Patrick lurched forward violently and threw his hands up to catch the front passenger's seat. Dmetri U-turned on a gravel lot and headed back to the classic car lot.

As soon as the car stopped, Patrick bolted out the back seat, waiting for the driver. He tried to remember some of the curse words Lilya used, but his anger held his thoughts captive. The driver's slow motions added to his rage. By the time he reached the rear of the car, Patrick's blood was boiling. Dmetri and Patrick were standing face to face, the showdown at hand, when, just as Patrick started to speak, a young female voice came from behind him.

"Can I help you gentleman?" The young woman looked up at Patrick, waiting for a response.

Patrick wanted to confront the smart-ass Russian driver.

"Yeah, give us a sec here, would ya?"

What he saw as he turned was a beautiful young girl with the longest red head of hair he'd ever seen. Patrick immediately forgot the driver and turned to the beauty.

"Hello, I'm Brigitte. I'm your service rep this morning. How can we help you Mr.—?"

"Connor, Patrick Connor. I'm interested in renting a car for a few days. Just stopped by to see if—"

Before Patrick could continue, he realized his driver had deposited his luggage on the pavement, the squeal of the Lincoln's tires the only indication his driver had left.

"I guess your driver was in a hurry?" said Brigitte.

"Yeah, he's Russian. I told him to stop so I could look at a car. I guess it ticked him off a little."

Patrick held his gaze on the young woman, realizing he appeared to be ogling her.

Patrick turned abruptly and pointed to the XKE. "I just want that baby for a few days."

"Sorry, but the Jag's taken. In fact, it's booked solid for the next month."

"You mean you put it out there just to tease us middle-aged guys?"

"Not at all. Everyone seems to want to rent it. Some people beg for just an hour. Something about the older classics that drive people crazy," she said with an air of formality that would've bothered him normally but not now.

"Kinda like you Irish girls with beautiful hair," Patrick said.

"Now you're gonna to make me blush."

"I doubt that. You probably get more stares than the Jag."

"I get some attention, but believe me, the Jag is the biggest beauty on this lot."

They continued their chat. Brigitte convinced Patrick to rent the only thing she could recommend, the Ford Explorer. A safe SUV, he probably wouldn't have to worry about breakdowns like most of the older cars. She'd let him have it for eighty dollars a day, plus insurance.

With small talk out of the way, Brigitte had a porter load Patrick's baggage. He was on his way to Montauk.

A smile broke across his face as he drove off the lot. A cute girl had helped him stay out of trouble with his Russian driver. I definitely don't want to mess with the Russians.

By the time Patrick drove through East Hampton, he realized he'd only had a single cup of airline coffee and a bagel all day. He was famished. His favorite breakfast place in the Hamptons was the Farmers Market.

The Farmers Market in Amagansett was probably far from a real farmers market. The shelves held some of the best wines, cheeses, and meats of any store in the Hamptons. The market not only represented Patrick's idea of food decadence for the rich, it also gave him one of the best stories he'd ever told about the area and its lifestyle.

Patrick told the story repeatedly, sure that over the years, the accuracy probably waned, but the theme and content of the story remained true.

While on vacation with family a few years back, Patrick made his morning trip to the Farmers Market for his typical breakfast, a large coffee, and a piece of fresh crumb cake.

As Patrick drove now, he tried to block the realities of home that awaited him in the Hamptons. The visit with his family brought heavy anxiety. A few miles more, down the Old Montauk Highway, and he'd be home, at least home to his condo. After a few hours of sleep, he'd face the family crisis.

Patrick shook his head to clear his agitation. He tried to focus on something pleasant and drifted back to his story about the Farmers Market. He recalled the story again in his head. *That's right,* Kill the time and amuse yourself with your silly stories about the Hamptons.

Patrick concentrated on that day at the Farmers Market. He stood in line, waiting to pay for his breakfast and nothing more on his mind than the quiet enjoyment of his coffee and cake as he sat outside in the cool shade—a typical morning in the Hamptons for him. As he waited, he read then reread the headlines of the New York Daily News and the New York Post, papers his wife prohibited in their home and but papers Patrick devoured with his coffee and cake.

Other than the clamor of the market, Patrick convinced himself the morning was off to a great start. Eager to get to the register, he noticed the checkout girl, new, obviously Irish, and very attractive. Patrick anticipated a little banter with the fresh face, typical middle-aged man, pining to be noticed by an attractive younger female.

Only one person ahead of him, Patrick waited patiently for his turn. What should I say to her? Maybe, "Where ya from, doll?" or, perhaps, "I can't believe this place consistantly finds the best looking Irish girls every summer!" Finally, the standard, "You know, the Farmers Market has won a contest for the past ten years running, having the best looking summer help in the Hamptons."

Patrick continued to gaze at the girl as she proceeded to check out the woman ahead of him. His suspense built as he got closer. He tried hard not to ogle too much, but she was a real looker. He barely noticed the customer she waited on.

As the woman proceded to check out in front of Patrick, the Irish lass prattled on with her pleasantries.

"Good morning, ma'am. Welcome to the Farmers Market."

The woman replied, "I know where I am, so you can cut the cute shit. My family and I live in the Hamptons every summer. I know I'm in the goddamn Farmers Market!"

The woman in front of him was a Jewish princess-type, condescending, bitchy, self-absorbed, obviously in a foul mood, and absolutely absent of any sense of humor. Patrick loved the Jews, but he pitied the poor soul on the receiving end of this bitch's wrath.

The young girl, taken aback, continued to check out the princess without any response.

"I really don't know why they can't hire Americans here—at least you can understand them."

"Pardon me now, ma'am?"

"Oh shit, you can't even understand English. Where do they get you people?"

"Well ma'am, I am from Ireland and I do understand English, but it's me second language, after Gaelic, of course."

"Gay what?"

"Gaelic, of course. Tis the official language of the people of Ireland."

"Look little miss-whoever-the-fuck-you-are, the only tongue I want is yours stuck in your little fresh mouth and get your pudgy little mick fingers busy checking out my groceries so my children don't starve this morning."

"Anything you say, ma'am."

"Hey, I told you to keep that little tongue in that Irish mouth of yours."

Patrick had heard enough. That princess was such a flaming cunt to the girl; he knew the princess wouldn't have said those things to a black or hispanic cashier. Political correctness, it seemed, only extended to people of color, not whites from Europe.

Patrick took a breath and began to speak in a pleasant, crisp Irish accent that would have charmed the panties off a nun. "You're the one who'd better watch the tongue while you talkin' to one of me own people. You need to learn to be civil. A little kindness would go a long way!"

"Oh fuck! All I need this morning is to be stuck between two micks in a goddamn debate."

"And another ting, young lady, we take great offense in takin' of the Lord's name in vain. I suppose in your country tis taken without much thought. But in Ireland, it's a great blasphemy," Patrick said.

"And what country do you think I'm from?" snapped the princess.

"Well I am only goin' to guess, but by your sweet disposition, the size of your nose, I am goin' to say that you're an Israelite," Patrick said, his voice full of cheer.

"You fucking anti-Semitic prick—how dare you? How fucking dare you?" screamed the princess.

"How dare I what?"

"I'm calling the manager and getting your fucking ass thrown out of this place."

"Let me tell you, my Irish arse will be here long after yours hits the street."

Now the rest of the market gathered around the checkout station. A manager hurried through the crowd, immediately recognizing Patrick.

"Mr. Connor, is there some type of problem here?"

"No. No problems, Jeff, really. It seems this lady in front of me is in a foul mood and wants to take her hate out on the rest of the world." Patrick delivered his accusations about the princess in a flat mid-Atlantic accent.

"What the fuck happened to your Irish accent?" screamed the princess.

"I believe it is going the same place you are, miss," Patrick said calmly with a smart-ass grin.

"And where is that, asshole?"

"It's being gone," said Patrick smugly.

The manager approached the woman, and said quietly, "Please leave before I call the police."

"Police!"

"Yes, the police. Take your groceries and leave," said the manager.

"And who the fuck is this asshole that he can stay?" demanded the princess.

"Lady, walk out of here while you're still able, without a police escort," said Patrick.

The princess turned to the checkout girl and said, "I'll remember you, you little Irish slut."

The manager walked up to the princess and simply said, "Now!"

"I have to pay."

"It's taken care of," replied the manager.

The princess gathered her groceries, shoveled them into her canvas shopping bag. She walked out the door, cursed under her breath.

The manager offered Patrick an apology. "Mr. Connor, I am truly sorry!"

"Hey, Jeff, sorry for what? She probably forgot to take her meds this morning and is a little out of sorts. Don't worry, you have a great little clerk here who handled the situation very well."

The manager walked away. Patrick chatted briefly with the young girl. "I had some good lines for you. You know the teasing kind about being pretty and all. But I guess I'll save them for next time."

"That was awfully nice of you. Not too many people would get involved like that."

They passed a few moments more as the morning checkout line grew. Patrick said goodbye and left.

Back to present reality, his wife and kids waited for him at the house. Patrick knew this may very well be his last trip back as a married man. He also realized his wife was serious about a divorce being civil, quiet, so as not to offend the sensibilities of the public lest the newspapers and gossip columnists picked up on it. It would require him

to sit and listen to her version of what had happened in
Washington over the last few months. Shameful as that
may be, the whole episode benefited their children. She'd
even considered removal of the Connor off their Whitt-
Connor last name. As Patrick drove on, he tried to
anticipate what his wife had in store.

Twenty minutes later, he reached his condo. He could
continue to obsess about what faced him in a few hours or
he could let it go for now. Patrick chose the later, turned on
the radio, his worries draining. The music was substandard,
but he cranked it up and focused on the road.

He slowed as he approached the sign that welcomed him
to the Village of Montauk. Montauk, the step-child of the
Hamptons. Folks often referred to the town as tawdry.
Patrick loved Montauk. He loved the people, their lack of
presumption, loved the beer joints, the cheap pizza parlors.
He loved it to spite the Hamptons' fine shops, fancy
restaurants, and, of course, it's tight-assed people. He
passed Village Pizza. Traditionally, he'd have stopped for a
couple of slices and a few beers, but not today. He wanted
to get to the manor, take a shower, catch a few hours sleep.

The advertisement brochures for Montauk Manor
described it as something out of The Great Gatsby. As
Patrick approached the resort off Harbor Road, the manor
did resemble grand decadence from the past. The tudor-
style white stucco structure stood out against the backdrop
of Long Island Sound did in fact resemble Gatsby's place.

Patrick had bought his condo coaxed by his father-in-
law, Jack, who explained the necessity of a man to have a
place of his own. Jack loved his late wife dearly, his
daughter, his world, but he was a realist and knew the
family tradition on his wife's side. The women dominated.
He'd learned this early on in his marriage. Jack carefully
ran the Whitt family business while at the same time eking
out something for himself too. Despite the Whitt wealth,

Jack Dausen amassed a small fortune on his own through wise investments in real estate.

Jack and Patrick were friends, more like brothers than in-laws. He knew Patrick and his daughter were unhappy together. He also saw his grandchildren weren't content with their father, under the influence of their mother's wicked tongue. He'd miss Jack. Almost as a second thought, told himself he'd miss his children too. Patrick felt no remorse for his absence in his kids' lives. They seemed more comfortable without him—at least, that's what he told himself. Since the death of their grandmother, the permanent move back to the Hamptons, and his wife's poisonous effect, Patrick's family operated best on their rigid schedule dictated by their mother.

The long corkscrew road served as the manor driveway. Patrick began to feel at home. He enjoyed his small condo and the solitude it provided when he visited. In fact, he felt a peacefulness at the manor he never revealed to anyone. There being no phone installed occasionally hindered the rental of the condo, but Patrick never needed the extra income; he preferred the isolation. The sequestered quiet was heavenly, if only for a few days.

Patrick pulled the Explorer up to the main entrance. Greeted by a young college student dressed in white shorts and red polo shirt with embroidered logo on the breast pocket, Patrick normally parked his own car and carried his own luggage, but this morning he chose valet. too tired to think.

The young man reached for the driver's door before Patrick actually stopped the car. The young man held on until the Explorer stopped. Patrick attempted a smart-ass remark but thought better of it when he saw the young man's face flushed with embarrassment. He let the young man open the car door.

"Welcome to Montauk Manor. Is this your first visit?"

"No, actually I'm an owner of one of the condos and just don't get around here much anymore."

"How long will you be staying with us Mr.—?"

"Connor, Patrick Connor. And cut the mister stuff. Pat or Patrick will do."

"Okay, Mr. Patrick, I mean Pat." Patrick handed the keys to the young man along with a five-dollar bill.

"Thank you, Pat." As almost an afterthought, the young man turned back to Patrick. "With a name like Patrick Connor, I take it you're Irish?"

"Yes I am. Why do you ask?"

"You know that Irish tavern down the road, O'Neil's?"

"Of course."

"Well they have this Irish singing group and—"

"I get the point," Patrick shot back to the young man. Patrick never liked to be dismissive of service help, especially in the Hamptons where dismissiveness was considered a high art form.

"I'm sorry. I didn't mean to be over-bearing. It's just that they're really good. They sing everything, not just the Irish stuff."

"Thanks for the advice and critique. If I get time, I'll try to check them out. Unfortunately, I'm on a tight schedule on this trip. My condo is five hundred four, so after you park the car please take care of the bags."

Patrick walked into the reception area. Protocol dictated he check in at the reception desk. Patrick took the elevator instead. He never cared for the check-in at his own condo. As a courtesy, he called the night before to make sure his condo wasn't occupied.

Calm diffused him as he entered his condo, a small and simple spa-like living space loaded with a wall of windows that flooded the condo with natural light, completed with an open chef's kitchen, airy living room, and welcoming bedroom. His bed was made up like the Waldorf Astoria, sheets turned down as requested. Wall decor consisted of various pictures of Long Island seascapes and landscapes. Patrick preferred no art rather than schlock art, but in order to rent the place, he needed a decorator's touch. A compromise had been reached on the television. Patrick wouldn't have it in the condo when he was in residence. If a guest requested one, management provided. A non-digital clock/radio was the only penetration from the outside world. He kept the radio in the living room on an end table. His bedroom was off limits for timepieces of any sort.

By the time Patrick reached his bed, he'd shed everything but his boxers. He preferred to take them off too, but reconsidered after he remembered the valet kid still had to deliver his bags. He collapsed on top of the covers and nestled his head into the pillow. Sleep came quickly. Patrick began to dream.

Patrick remembered the dream sequence and tried to replay them over the next few weeks, as if they gave him a clue as to what had gone on with Lilya.

Dream 1:

Lilya in Moscow, she and a friend, in a nightclub on Buskin Street. The club, dim and dirty. Lilya and her friend drank straight vodka. No men at the bar, only women. Drinks were all-you-can-drink free, for the ladies. The two friends celebrated Lilya's good fortune, her selection by a prestigious American university to study medical business practices. Her friend told her about American men, how they liked to fuck.

"They want you on the bottom so they can control you," the friend said.

Lilya threw back her head and laughed. "No man can control me!" she screamed. "When I fuck, I fuck the way I want to fuck!"

Both women laughed, downed more vodka. The bar was filled with young women, all in various stages of drunkenness.

"Where are our men?" Lilya demanded.

"We want men," the bar room chanted.

A large black African man appeared on stage. He wore a colorful native costume and a devilish mask over his face. In his hand, he had a large fake rubber spear. As he danced, he used his spear like a giant penis, dangling it between his legs, making long stroking motions with his hands. He removed his loincloth and uncovered a maxed-out g-string that barely secured his horse-like penis. The crowd squealed with delight—they wanted to see his package. They lusted after him to use his "spear."

A young girl appeared on stage. The crowd began to cheer. The girl was Polish and very drunk. With the ladies' encouragement, the young girl attempted to take the African's g-string off. The African made a fast dance move and foiled her advances. Her second attempt was successful. His large black penis was now fully erect. The crowd roared their approval. The Polish girl began to stroke the dancer's large cock. He motioned her to come closer. She moved so her crotch was next to the dancer's. She began to grind with his. The crowd rumbled that they'd never seen such a gigantic cock. The dancer pushed the Polish girl down by her shoulders until her face was in front of his cock.

Her blonde hair contrasted against his large blackness. He was so huge he was able to wave it on both sides of her head and still have several inches go past her light hair.

The women screeched for the girl to put the cock in her mouth. She turned, smiled, and revealed several missing teeth in the front of her mouth.

She took the African's cock into her mouth then pulled the cock out off her mouth, again smiling toward the audience. This time all of her teeth were missing. The raucous group laughed at her ugliness, chanted for her to fuck the African.

"She is such a stupid Pollock," someone yelled.

"Fuck the African, you dumb ugly bitch," the crowd yelled.

The Polish girl stood up, faced the crowd, smiled again, and as she pulled down her skirt. She wore no panties.

Someone yelled out, "Just like a Pollock. Always dressed for work."

The African came up behind her, bent her over like a rag doll, held her by the hips, and waited for the crowd's command.

"Fuck her! Fuck her, you black devil!"

"Fuck her! She's a dumb Polish bitch!"

"Fuck her dumb Polish ass!"

The African pushed forward with his penis. The Polish girl's mouth opened to scream. She couldn't scream because a large black snake in the shape of the African's cock came out of her mouth.

The crowd screamed.

The African pushed the lifeless Polish girl into the crowd and began to dance.

Dream Two:

Lilya laughed at the sight of the dead Polish girl on the floor. She turned to the stage to watch the African dance some more. He pulled Lilya on the stage, and she began dancing with him. She turned to the audience and the African came up behind her as he did the dead Polish girl.

The crowd came to life. Lilya smiled at the cheers.

"Fuck her and kill her like you did the Polish bitch!"

"Fuck and kill, fuck and kill," the crowd roared.

The African pushed Lilya over and penetrated her. Lilya screamed. The African laughed with the crowd. Lilya screamed louder. The African's hands turned to hooves, his head and neck into a goat. His large black goat head was now on Lilya's back. His large cock turned thin, pink, and ejaculated on her nude white back.

The crowded screamed with joy.

The goat head backed up, admired what he had just done, and began to lick the semen from her back.

The goat creature pushed Lilya's lifeless body into the crowd.

Patrick lurched out from his sleep and shook his head violently as if to knock the dream from his brain and body. He sat up and ran his hand over the bed. Lilya wasn't there. He remembered where he was and realized it was just a dream. No, a nightmare. Patrick hadn't dreamt for years, let alone a full-scale nightmare.

He reached for the clock on the night stand. He needed the time and date immediately. Again he reminded himself where he was, in the Hamptons at his retreat. Phones and clocks were banned. He rolled out of his king-size bed and staggered into the living room.

His need to know the time right then overwhelmed him. Certain he'd missed the meeting with his wife, he imagined the look on her face if he drove up a day late for their meeting. He knew the marriage was over, but he didn't want it to end on a sour note. "Drunk again, are we?" Or better yet, "Still can't keep a promise or an appointment."

Patrick made it from the bedroom to the living room in search of his radio clock. He'd picked it up at a garage sale for five dollars. The clock, ancient, actually had hands and a face, no digital shit. A bit of a 1950s relic, it comforted him. He only wished in that moment it was still evening, not morning. The display read 6:47. But a.m. or p.m., he didn't know. Patrick turned on the radio. He knew if he heard Howard Stern, he was screwed. Baseball, any baseball would be good. He heard the announcer's call of the starting line-up for the Yankee's game against the White Sox. Relief swept over him like a cool breeze in the desert. He laughed to himself and started back to the bedroom for a shave and shower. His bags had been left in the living room. He retrieved his toiletries.

Patrick skipped the shave to save time. After a shower and change of clothes, he entered the lobby and asked the desk clerk to have someone bring his car up. The clerk pushed a buzzer. The same young man from earlier in the day appeared.

"Hi, Mr. Connor, I mean Pat. I hope I didn't wake you when I put the bags in the room."

"I wish you had," Patrick muttered.

"Excuse me?"

"Nothing, just talking to myself again. Comes with age, I guess."

Patrick waited for the Explorer. Rather than rehearse his conversation with his wife, his mind drifted toward his dreams. He remembered Lilya talking about a terrible place she'd visited in Moscow called the Hungry Duck. She'd gone there on several occasions with friends. She also told him about the fantasy she'd had about the old night guard in the dormitory. A highly erotic dream, but frightening. He was debating whether to discuss the dream with Lilya when the valet walked up with his keys. Patrick reached for his wallet to get the kid a tip.

"Oh, not needed. You took care of me earlier and that was good enough."

"Okay" was the only thing Patrick could muster.

"Just another reminder for you to stop and see the Irish Angels down at O'Neil's. That is, if you have the time."

"Probably not this trip, but thanks for the tip."

"I think it's their last night."

"Well, thanks. You must be a real fan."

Patrick practiced in his mind what he would discuss with his wife as he drove out of the driveway and made his way up to Village of Montauk on the Harbor Road. He still loved his wife, he knew any type of relationship that resembled a marriage was now out of the question. He also realized he actually feared his wife, much as he did his mother-in-law—the inherent power they possessed to intimidate men.

Early in their marriage, his young wife had made fun of the long lineage of dominant women in the Whitt family, the way they controlled men. Told him to "shoot her" if she ever acted or sounded like her mother. Patrick never reminded her of her words. She'd have denied saying it, anyway, would have orated a long defense of her saintly mother, how her mother's life, ever dedicated to the preservation of the Whitt heritage and fortune, benefitted them. Patrick never developed the stomach to fight with his wife.

The kids, almost grown, were virtual strangers to him. The estate and business holdings had to be figured into a divorce. Patrick decided he wanted nothing, just to walk away. However, he realized it wouldn't be easy. The divorce would be finalized only after months of paperwork by the Whitt family bankers and lawyers.

The road sign told him to brake for a railroad crossing. The portable sign next to it on the roadside interrupted his thoughts:

Straight from Ireland
The Irish Angels Singers
Last Night

Patrick slowed for the railroad tracks, giving himself an excuse to turn into O'Neil's parking lot.

O'Neil's Tavern was what most Americans who hadn't been to Ireland thought a real Irish pub looked like. Old wood furniture mixed and matched from pubs all over Ireland. Pictures of Irish poets and, playwrights adorned the wall. The obligatory map of Ireland over the bar was courtesy of Budweiser beer. The stench of stale beer and acrid smoke choked the air.

It took Patrick's eyes a moment to adjust to the dim lighting. When he finally could see, he headed straight for the bar. The bartender was in his late thirties with thinning red-blond hair and a ruddy Irish complexion, the result of too many shots of Jameson's.

"A pint of Guinness, please," Patrick ordered.

The bartender poured. Patrick began to talk.

"I understand you've got an Irish singing group here tonight," said Patrick.

"I'm afraid not. The guy who rents the sign was supposed to take it away today. Last night was the last night they were going to sing."

"So I missed them, I guess."

"Yes and no. Some of the girls are here now. The rest are out back in the cottages. They'll come over for dinner in a few minutes and you can see them all."

"Are they as good as everyone says?" Patrick relied on testimony of the valet at the manor.

"No, they're much better than anyone could ever try to explain." Patrick actually felt a slight feeling of remorse that he'd missed the show.

"Tell you what," offered the bartender. "Take your pint over to their table and just say hello. That's all it takes, and trust me, you'll be entertained for hours. By the way, are you Irish?"

"Yes I am," said Patrick proudly.

"Well, forget the hour of entertainment. If you're Irish they take a liking to you—the entertainment could last for days!"

The bartender gave Patrick a knowing wink as he handed him his pint.

Patrick took his Guinness and made his way across the wooden dance floor toward the back tables. Halfway to his destination, Patrick heard a shrill voice rise from the table.

"Well if ya gonna take a day to get here we might as well find another gentleman to entertain."

Patrick stopped and looked behind him to see who she talked to.

"I'm talking to you. There's no one else in the damn place. Just keep walking, and we won't bite ya too hard."

In the dark corner, Patrick came upon four women in a booth. Each had a drink in front of them and a cigarette burning between their fingers.

"That bartender sent you back to bother us, didn't he?"

Before Patrick could reply, another voice said, "Nina, for God's sake, we'll never trap a man tonight if you go and scare 'em all off."

Patrick, now in front of the booth, took a closer look at the ladies.

"So you're the Irish Angels?"

"Not tonight, sweetie. We're in too wicked a mood to be angels, but if you buy the next round we'll let you sit with us and listen to our gossip."

Patrick took a chair from a nearby table and slid it up to the head of the booth. The singers had just finished off a legitimate tour of the US. The ladies' manager had made a deal with the owner of O'Neil's, an hour show per night, three or four nights a week, free room and board. The women enjoyed the beach during the day. With their final show the night before, they just wanted to relax and have a little fun.

The group had paid for a professional manager to set up their American tour. He was now back in Ireland. The women were now on their own except for the leadership of Nina, the woman who howled at Patrick. She explained her position as the "road mother" to the girls; she took care of the personal lives both on the road and in Ireland. Her day job back home was a pharmacist.

Patrick recounted the purpose of his visit, to tie up some family business. He omitted details related to his wife or the divorce. He'd keep the dirty laundry in the closet. Doing family business sounded legitimate enough.

Four more gals joined the group. With tables pushed together, Patrick was suddenly surrounded by eight happy beauties.

Nina introduced each one. Patrick couldn't keep up with all their names; they all sounded like Mary, Helen, Megan, and Ann. He remembered Nina's name—she was the most talkative and most attractive.

"Will ya join us for dinner, Patrick?" asked Nina.

"No thanks. I got to get to East Hampton and finish some business."

"East Hampton, now—would you live in one of those big homes we saw coming in here?"

"Yes, the family has a big home, but it's not on the main road, it has a beach front."

"A beach front," one of the girls responded.

"It's okay, but I very seldom get to use it due to work schedules and the like." Patrick hated to sound stuffy or formal. He wanted to tell the ladies the truth but not bore them with his problems.

"Well, if you won't eat with us, you'll let me buy you another Guinness, won't you now?" offered Nina.

Patrick glanced at the wall clock, half past seven. One more pint. He'd be on his way to the house in no time and be a little loose for the anticipated confrontation with his wife.

"Okay, one more and I really have to be out of here." Nina raised her hand and the bartender came to the table.

"Give us a round of our usual and give the handsome man next to me another pint of Guinness, would you please."

Some young waitresses brought the food to the table. It was served family style with the plates, bowls, and silverware passed around. Patrick glanced at the food that seemed to be a variation of American bar food with a hint of Irish accent.

Patrick's pint arrived with the last platter of food. He began to notice his stomach growling and remembered he hadn't eaten since his airplane bagel and a cup of black coffee. He thought about Nina's offer for a bite of food, but opted for his pint instead.

Patrick watched with amazement as the women ate and chatted around the table. All of them were do-able, a few gorgeous, and the rest, well, pleasant enough.

One girl caught his interest with her unusual mannerisms. She didn't eat, only sipped her drink. When the rest of the girls laughed, she suppressed her laugh, covering her mouth. Odd.

Patrick asked Nina about her. "Nina, the girl at the end, with the white blouse, she seems shy, reserved, more than the other girls."

"Shy and reserved compared to the rest of us—most people consider her normal, the rest of us crazy!"

Patrick felt rebuffed. Maybe he'd asked something too personal.

But Nina continued, "To be honest with you, Patrick, she is a bit on the shy side. She likes to eat off by herself and she seldom laughs with rest of us."

"Why's that?"

"Well, if you stay around for at least one song, I'll show you why."

"Now you have piqued my curiosity. Could you at least give me a little hint?"

Nina's voice lowered and she shifted her chair to be closer to Patrick. "Well you've noticed how shy she is. There is a reason. Have you noticed she covers her mouth when she tries to laugh? Seems she's got a bad case of crooked teeth. Her mouth looks like a picket fence after a cyclone."

Nina paused for effect and gave Patrick a moment to stare down the table toward the girl.

"But along with her crooked teeth, God gave her the most beautiful voice in all of Ireland. A few years back, she was runner up in our Euro-Vision contest. You know, the show that started the River Dance phenomenon? Anyway, she was up for the top prize and the damn cameraman did a close-up of her mouth and if you can believe the rumors, people actually turned off their TVs."

"Why doesn't she get braces or something?" asked Patrick.

"She is a deeply religious girl and feels if God wanted her to have straight teeth she would have been born that way. She feels if she ever got her teeth straightened, God would take away her voice."

"You're kidding me, right?" asked Patrick.

"No, Patty, I am not kidding nor am I kidding about her singing talents. You will never hear a more beautiful voice in your life and that's for sure and for certain. Her songs have a magical spell about them."

Patrick was enough of an Irishman to understand what Irish referred to as blarney and what the rest of the world knows as bullshit.

"Like I said, Nina, I've got to get home—" He stared off at the wall clock.

"Patty, one song, just stay for one song," Nina pleaded.

"Okay, okay, but only because you tell me she's that good," said Patrick.

"Good is not a strong enough word to describe her. Pick your song, Patty."

"*Danny Boy*," shouted Patrick.

A very audible groan drifted from the table. "What's the problem, doesn't she know the song?" asked Patrick.

"Does she know it?" replied Nina. "It's her very best song, but it is definitely a closer, so to speak. She tries to slate it as the last song of the evening."

"Why's that?" asked Patrick.

"Be patient, Patty."

"Mary Ann, our distinguished guest would like to hear you sing—would you mind?"

The young woman covered her mouth and shook her head in the affirmative.

"And of course you've heard his request."

The young woman stood up. She seemed to be taller than the rest of the group and slimmer. Even with the white blouse and knee-length skirt, Patrick could see she had a beautiful body. Her face was milky white, her lips full. He found himself drawn to her.

She opened her mouth and began to sing.

Two sensations came over Patrick. His eyes focused on the grotesqueness of her crooked teeth, but his ears were invaded by and flooded with the most beautiful voice he had ever heard.

The bartender rushed to the table and stood behind Nina and Patrick.

By the time she reached...

"The summer's gone and all the flowers are a dying"

the bartender was mopping his nose with his sleeve.

Patrick closed his eyes, enjoyed the music.

"And if you come when all the flowers are dying
and I'm dead as dead I well be
You'll come and find a the place where I am lying
and kneel and say an 'Ave' there for me."

The image of Patrick's mother and Father Peat came to mind. Patrick thought they were with him in the bar. Afraid to open his eyes, he let the notes pierce his soul.

The bartender sobbed as, finally...

"I simply sleep in peace until you come to me."

Patrick pulled a dinner napkin off the table and enveloped his wet face, releasing his emotions.

The bartender wept and clapped his hands. "This is the fourth night I've heard her sing that song ,and it still breaks me up."

"Girls, drinks are on the house," snivelled the bartender.

The bartender retired to his post. Nina gave Patrick a moment to compose himself.

"Who did you see?" asked Nina, matter of factly.

"What do you mean?"

"You know what I mean, when she sings that song all men react the same way. They all cry. But some others swear they see someone who's passed on. That is why we call it our closer, because after she sings it, you want to close the bar and go home."

"I saw my mother and a priest who was my guardian when I was a kid," Patrick said.

"But you really did see them, right?" Nina asked now forcefully.

"Yes, damn it, I saw them!"

"Take it easy, Patty. It's just one of those Irish things, that's all. When Mary Ann sings, it's as if heaven opens up and all the people we love come to hear. For some reason, it's more pronounced when she sings Danny Boy. So I know you thought this 'gift from God' stuff was a bunch of blarney. Now you'll have something to tell your grandkids."

The bartender sent a waitress over with the round he bought for the table. The young girl placed the Guinness in front of Patrick. He almost pushed it away but instead took a big swallow and then another until he emptied the glass.

"You got a thirst there tonight don't ya, Patty?" Nina said.

"Yeah, I guess so."

"Patty, one thing, that girl has some gift from God. In all the times she's sung with us, people never have told of seeing people who have passed on and done them harm. Are ya hearing me, Patty? The only people they see are the good people in their lives, the people who are surely in heaven."

Patrick reached for the napkin on the table to blot his eyes again. He held up his empty glass for the server. This time he didn't look at the clock on the wall.

He turned back to Nina. "The bartender. What does he see?"

"Nothing," said Nina. "He's just a sentimental cry baby and loves the song."

The girls at the far end of the table began to sing, and someone shouted, "Reply time!"

"What's reply time?"

"Oh, it's a little game we play amongst ourselves. You know, someone sings a few bars from a song and someone else has to sing back a reply from another song that deals with something from the first song. Whoever gets the most first replies wins."

"Sounds simple enough," said Patrick.

A girl in the middle of the table began to sing.

"Hello, Dolly, hello, Dolly, it's so nice to have you back where you belong"

Patrick shot up his hand. He cleared his throat:

"Isn't it odd, isn't queer, they just made me, from my mother's left ear.
Bring on the clones, where are the clones"

Half the table began to clap. The girl who sang the song looked bewildered. "What does that have to do with Hello Dolly?"

"The cloned sheep, you twit. The sheep that was cloned in Scotland, her name was Dolly," Nina yelled back in a scolding voice.

The next tune was from an obscure musical Patrick had never heard of. Nina cupped her hand over his ear and in a loud whisper said, "You're a very sharp man. What type of work do you do?"

Patrick considered his standard "whoremaster" but thought better of it.

"I do consulting work for government officials."

He relaxed, enjoying the music and the company. The divorce talk with his wife could wait. Another pint appeared. A girl at the end of the table waved to him as the waitress placed the cold glass in front of him and he drank it.

Patrick noticed two things about Nina. The more he drank, the closer she moved toward him, the more questions she asked about his house by the sea.

"You say you can walk out your back door and take a dip in the ocean anytime you wish?" she asked.

"Anytime the water is warm enough. The waters of the North Atlantic are like Ireland, cold and unforgiving," he said.

"Kinda like a wife, would you say, now Patty?"

Nina looked directly at Patrick and winked. "Tell me, did you ever take you clothes off and jump into the ocean naked?"

"Not lately, but a few years back, I was known to do things like that," he said.

"There's nothing like trying to recapture the old youth, is there?" She stroked Patrick's inner thigh.

Patrick finally managed to look at the wall clock. It was ten thirty. He knew he was drunk, too drunk to drive, not too drunk to comprehend he should try to get home this evening. Patrick rose from the table and excused himself to the restroom.

When he returned, there were only five of the sixteen Angels at the table. Nina was still in her seat and the singer, Mary Ann, was next to her.

"Tell you what, Patty. We been talking and thinking, thinking and talking and what we have come up with is that we want to see ya house by the sea." Nina was obviously drunk, her words labored.

Patrick, also drunk, was in an unusually arrogant mood. He wanted to take the women home, show them his house by the sea. He wanted to confront his wife, tell her how she was the one who'd changed, from a fun-loving college girl into a miserable shrew like her mother. Finally, he wanted Nina. She'd played up to him from the moment she saw him, flirted all night; now he wanted to see if she'd pay off.

Before Patrick responded, Nina added, "And by the way, Patty, I've ordered a round of drinks to go."

The group left the bar and stood out in the parking lot next to the Explorer.

Patrick surveyed the group. Like him, they'd all had too much to drink, except the singer, Mary Ann. She'd nursed her soda water all night.

"Mary Ann," slurred Patrick. "Can you drive a car?"

Out of apparent habit, she covered her mouth before she answered. "I think I can, I mean I do drive back home, but I'm afraid to drive on the wrong side of the road like you Americans do."

"What if you didn't have to drive on the road? What if you could drive on a straight line, could you do it then?" asked Patrick.

"Patty, what the hell you have in mind?" asked Nina.

Patrick dug in his pockets, fished for his keys, and handed them to Mary Ann.

Instinctively, Mary Ann opened the passenger's side and stared. She almost asked where the wheel was but Nina corrected her.

"Try the other side, dear," said Nina.

Nina pulled herself into the passenger's seat and the other three women got into the back seat. Patrick stood in the parking lot as he waited for an invitation.

"As passengers we sure as hell can't go to your house without you, now can we?"

Patrick paused before he spoke. He wanted to say something clever, but nothing came. He was wasted. That frightened him.

Nina motioned him into the front seat. Both squeezed into the bucket seat until Nina adjusted herself and was on Patrick's lap.

"Now, if you dare tell me that me arse is too big, you're gonna be walking home."

"No, no," he said.

"What road do I take?" asked Mary Ann.

"Go right when you leave the parking lot. Take the railroad tracks to East Hampton."

"What?" squawked Mary Ann "You want me to drive on the railroad tracks?"

"Listen to the man," said Nina. "He told you that you could drive straight down the road in the middle."

The girls in the back seat giggled.

Mary Ann understood she'd have no allies in her protest.

The end of the Long Island Railroad tracks lay adjacent to O'Neil's parking lot. The gravel gave way to pavement and the pavement turned to rail ties and gravel. Mary Ann tried to oversteer and hit the tracks. The Explorer lurched from one side to the other.

Nina yelled, "Keep the fooking car in the middle!"

Mary Ann complied, and within a few hundred yards, the SUV seemed to right itself.

"Would you listen to that?" said Nina. "The tires are almost singing as they hit the ties."

The girls in the back seat started and stopped a few songs. Before long, they begged Mary Ann to sing for them.

"Mary Ann, the only way you are going to get them to shut up is to sing to the babies. Isn't that right, Patty?"

Nina nudged Patrick's ribcage with her elbow and only received a grunt back.

"Oh, it seems we have a real live one here, ladies. Maybe we can pick up a spare on the way."

The girls laughed, and Nina asked Mary Ann if she would lead them in an appropriate song.

"What song would be appropriate?" Mary Ann asked.

"Think girl, we are in America, driving down a railroad track like any other American."

Mary Ann placed her left hand in front of her mouth, and gently cleared her throat.

"I hear that train a coming, coming around the ben'
I haven't seen the sunshine in I don't know when
I'm stuck here in Folsom Prison and time keeps marching on."

"Good choice, good choice," yelled Nina over Mary Ann and the harmony from the back seat. "You sound like June Carter herself, and what's her husband's name again?"

Patrick did notice Mary Ann's voice was deeper and more husky then her regular soprano voice. He noticed this immediately before he passed out.

After "Chattanooga Choo-Choo" and "I've Been Working on the Railroad," Nina held up her hand and said, "Hold on for a second, would ya now, girls?. I think we are in this East Hampton place. At least that sign said so at the station. Let's pull off of the tracks and get on a real road and try to find lover boy's house by the sea."

Mary Ann turned left as soon as she reached a rail crossing and was on a solid surface for the first time in about twenty-five minutes.

"Just stay to the right and you'll be okay," instructed Nina.

Mary Ann kept the Explorer at a steady twenty miles per hour as she searched for some signs of life in the Village of East Hampton.

"I see lights up ahead—perhaps it's a village."

"Look, there is a constable or something up ahead," shouted one of the girls from the back seat. "Stop and get some directions or we'll be driving all night."

The Explorer crept up to a young man with a tan uniform and police nightstick in his hand.

Nina spoke for the group. "Good evening, sir, we got a bit of a problem here. You see, our friend here has had too much to drink and we promised we'd get him home."

Nina realized what she thought was a young man actually was a boy of no more than seventeen or eighteen years old. The boy stepped up to the vehicle with his nightstick in both hands trying his best to show that he did have some authority over the situation.

"Has your driver been drinking?" His voice was light, almost girlish.

"Oh, for heaven's sake, no! Mary Ann never drinks. As for the rest of us, well, we're pretty much in our cups."

Nina shifted her body so she could get off of Patrick's lap and maneuver the door lever. The Explorer's door opened and the young boy jumped back to the curb. As Nina exited the vehicle, she observed the boy backed further away.

"Oh I didn't mean to startle you, son."

"You should always tell an officer when you're leaving a vehicle. Had this been a gun—"

"Oh, I'm sorry but me legs are tired and my friends are drunk. We just need some directions."

"What is your friend's name?"

"He is Mr. Patrick Connor. Would you know him, now?"

"Oh yes, he's married to the Whitt lady. The Whitts have the biggest house in East Hampton, probably the entire Hamptons. And you say that's Mr. Connor, I mean the man whose lap you were sitting on, that's him?"

Nina was drunk, but in the years on the road with the Angels, she'd learned to be diplomatic at the right moments.

"Oh lad, it's not what you think. Mr. Connor, that's Patty, and we're cousins. We share the same grandfather. It's just we were in town and he had a little bit too much to drink." Nina's voice trailed off as she studied the young man's face.

"You're his cousin, really?"

"I swear on our dead grandfather's grave!"

"Okay, how can I help you folks? I mean if you want to get to the Whitt Estate, I can certainly give you directions."

Nina cut the boy off with, "Oh directions would be grand, but maybe you could come with us and show us how to get there?"

The boy stood quietly for a moment. "Well technically, I'm off work now. I'm a summer auxiliary officer."

"Grand, you can come with us and when it's time to leave we'll get you home by taxi."

The boy climbed in the back seat. One of the girls sat on her neighbor's lap to make room for the new guest.

Mary Ann continued to drive. She had to quiet the crowd on several occasions because the chatter rose too high that she couldn't hear the directions from the young constable.

Within ten minutes, they sat before the entrance to the Whitt Estate.

"Here you are. The biggest place in the Hamptons," the boy said.

"Bless the cradle of the Christ child," Nina said aloud to herself.

Even in the dark of the evening, the Whitt estate's opulence was obvious. Give it a full moon, the backdrop of the ocean, and it was something from a dream.

Patrick woke briefly. He realized where he was and said two words: "Carriage House."

"Pat, Pat, get up. It's time to go!" The voice was familiar to Patrick as well as the surroundings, but who was it and where was he? Patrick opened his eyes slowly, and the blur from the night before came into focus for him.

He was in the Whitt carriage house. Over the bed was none other than his father-in-law, Jack Dausen.

"Pat, it's about nine thirty in the morning. You had some guests last night. Dawn saw the SUV when she walked the dogs. She thought it was you. She entered the carriage house. Several naked women were here and a young boy partially clothed, and you were in this bed with a woman. She was naked, but you were dressed. Dawn woke them up, called a cab. The boy's mother thought of pressing charges. Seems he's only eighteen. He's some type of summer help for the police in the village."

Jack shut up and withdrew in silence for a moment.

"Goddamn it, Pat, It could have been simple. My daughter wants a divorce and she wanted to sit down yesterday, talk as adults, and you have to show up like this. Look, I'll make it simple. Dawn wants you off the property. I didn't find any luggage in the Explorer. Figured you'd stopped by the manor first. I took the liberty of calling them to get your things ready."

Jack Dausen turned and headed toward the main door of the carriage house. He turned for one last look. "Pat, I know things have not been good. I will always love you as a son, but if you need help, get it, for your sake."

Doc's Bar

Paulie waited for his friend Mick in front of the new bar on Forty-Seventh and Second Avenue. Doc's had the latest theme bar to hit the Manhattan tavern scene. The motif was modeled after an emergency room. Both waiters and waitresses wore powder blue scrubs. The drink menu took the hospital schtick to the next level with cocktails like the Car Wreck, Very Bloody Mary, and Absolut Abortion.

The concept had been birthed from some doctors in the city who had too money and little business sense. Despite the weird theme, the bar was a hit amidst the medical community.

Paulie was a third-year resident at City Hospital.

His specialty was tissue rejection from transplants. He enjoyed his work and looked forward to a long medical career in research. Research may not garner the impressive salary of a surgeon, but a piece of flesh wouldn't call him at three in the morning. His three-hundred-thousand-dollar student loans loomed over his head like a dark cloud. Med school was not cheap, and in New York living expenses were outrageous.

Paulie checked his watch for the second time. He wanted to call Mick to remind him, but decided against it. Mick always managed a wise-ass remark when Paulie questioned him about time.

"What's the matter, Jew boy? You chargin' me by the hour or what?"

Mick Ryan and Paulie Pepper had been best friends from kindergarten through college. Mick went off to law school at Loyola and Paul stayed in the city to attend Columbia med school. They stayed in touch but had drifted apart after Paulie changed his name from Pepper to Schlepperchov.

As Catholic school boys on Long Island, Paul had confided to Mick that his grandfather had come from

Russia in 1903 and changed the family name from Schlepperchov to Pepper. His reason: "It's hard enough for a Russian to make it in America, but a Russian Jew?"

The first words out of Mick's mouth when he found out Paulie was Jewish were, "Hey, Paulie. You know why Jews have such big noses?"

Before Paul could answer, Mick responded to his own question. "Cause air's free!"

Both boys laughed, but from then on Mick always had a Jew joke for Paulie.

After he completed his undergraduate work, Paulie took a year off to travel. He visited Russia, traveling to his grandfather's home outside of St. Petersburg. He actually met some distant relatives, the few that were left. Through a translator, they told of the family history, of the pogroms carried out by the Cossacks in the czarist times. They also recounted the discrimination that continued under the Soviets. After Russia, Paulie visited Israel and got in touch with his "Jewish side" as he called it.

Coming back to the States, he informed his parents and friends he planned to convert to Judaism and change his last name back to Schlepperchov.

His Irish mother cried. His Jewish father congratulated him and promised to go to temple with him.

When he told his friend Mick, his first response was, "Oh, great, now I can call you Christ killer, that's okay. Right?"

Paul was checking his watch for a third time when the cab door slammed shut, breaking his concentration.

Mick Ryan hopped the curb and talked before Paulie could say hello.

"Jesus Christ, are we ever gonna get fuckin' English-speaking people driving cabs in this goddamn city? I mean, this rag head took the slow route when I told him specifically to take the FDR. I mean, can't these fuckers ever get it right?"

Again before Paulie could answer, Mick rattled off the latest merger he was involved in.

"You gotta start making money, Kikey, so I can steer you in to some real good investments. I mean, you are my beard for some real fuckin' good stuff, right?"

Paulie listened, waiting for a pause in his friend's chatter as they walked toward the bar entrance.

"So what kinda place is this, anyways?" Mick asked.

Paulie finally got a word in as they entered the tavern.

"It's a place set up by a group of doctors. Check it out."

As the friends entered the bar they were greeted by an attractive hostess in a white nurse's uniform—not the type to be found in any hospital—with an old-fashioned nurse's cap.

"The bar or lounge, gentleman?"

Mick looked at the pretty young blond, peeked at her breasts on display like a dessert tray on top of her dress.

"I really feel sick. Can I get mouth to mouth to mouth or what?"

The young waitress rolled her eyes as Paulie simply said, "The bar will be fine."

The young faux nurse directed them to the left.

Strolling through the common area that separated the two parts of the bar, they were greeted by medical examination lamps, crash carts, and ancient wheel chairs causally arranged against the white tile and light green walls.

"Holy shit, this place reminds me of a fuckin' emergency room!" Mick said.

"That's why the place is called Doc's. The lounge the Recovery Room and the bar the Emergency Room."

"One thing," Paulie whispered. "Please keep the Kikey shit to a minimum. Probably half this place is Jewish and it could be hazardous to your health."

Mick seemed to ignore his friend's warning and came back with, "Oh yeah, I am so sure some little Hymmie's gonna kick my ass!"

"Please, there are some Israeli doctors in here. They're all military too, and yes, they will severely kick your ass and probably mine too."

This time, Mick seemed to get the message. An attractive lady with short black hair approached from behind the bar and asked for their orders.

"Hey, babe, cute accent," Mike said. "Where you from? Russia or something?"

"I'm Israeli," she said coldly.

"Oh, really, and are you part of the Israeli army?" Mick asked in a mocking tone.

"Yes, of course. All young Israelis are in the armed forces."

"What are you, a nurse or something?"

"No, actually I am a major in special forces and a doctor. I'm here in New York at NYU graduate school studying trauma surgery on fellowship."

Paulie cut in. "Now that my friend has your résumé perhaps we can have a few drinks?"

"Two Jameson's neat, and make them doubles."

"Well at least you didn't order Mogen David. Glad you still got half the Irish in you."

"Mick, give it a rest, okay?"

"Okay, okay, I'll try. So how's it going? Are you ready to do some real investing?"

"I need to get this year over with and start making real money. I mean eighty grand a year as a resident just doesn't cut it in the big city."

"Tell me about it! I'm at a quarter of a mill, and I still wonder where it goes. I mean——." Mick cut himself off and turned his head to the left of the bar. "Oh my God, and that's my God and not yours. Check this out!

Three chairs down, a petite blond placed her laptop on the bar. Engaged in a heated conversation on her cell phone, she concluded with "Paka, paka."

Mick turned to Paulie. "I know she's a Russian. 'Paka, paka' is the same as bye bye, right?"

"You're right, she's a Russian. She's also a MD. She's here to study for her American boards. She's here every day."

"Every day?"

"Yeah, she's got quite the history. In layman terms, you could call her a nympho-maniac. She's got to have it every day."

"Okay, okay. How do you know so much? Did you bang her, or what?"

"No, the little Israeli behind the bar is more my type. The Russians are a little too wild for me."

"So you stick with the members of your tribe, right?"

"Sometimes, but after a couple of twenty-four-hour shifts, the only thing you want out of a bed is sleep."

"What the fuck has med school turned you into, a eunuch, for Christ sake?"

"No, but you learn to appreciate sleep more than ever."

"Enough about your sleep deprivation—tell me more about the little girl next to us. My God, she looks like a gymnast or something. The possibilities, the possibilities."

"Well, let me tell you a little more. She's very picky. She gets hit on all the time. Takes the guy's name. If she likes him, they meet up the next day, go to her apartment, do the dirty."

"So what's her type?"

"I don't know. She has no type, only quality." Paulie said.

A slight man in a black leather jacket approached the Russian doctor and handed her a white envelope. They didn't speak—only nodded heads and he walked away.

"By the way, supposedly that happens every day. Someone comes to the bar, hands her an envelope, and leaves," reported Paulie.

"What the hell's in the envelope?" asked Mick.

"Don't know. Some people say its material for the USMLE that she's studying for."

"The what?"

"Sorry. United States Medical Licensing Examination. It's a three-part test foreign doctors or US citizens who have gone to offshore medical schools have to take. I understand it's a bitch to pass."

"Can't be that hard with all the fucking foreigners we have practicing medicine in America. I mean the number of fuckin' foreign doctors has to outnumber our cab drivers. Right?"

"One other thing—she's allergic to latex. She can't use condoms."

"Fuck. That's all I need is some Russian twat giving me the clap or worse."

"But hear me out. Supposedly, she will not have sex with a guy without doing a blood test. I mean, she actually has a little lab in her apartment where she analyzes the blood. She also gives the guys a pretty good going-over for things like warts, herpes, and chlamydia."

"What the fuck? You mean she does the swab up the cock thing?"

"Oh, I see you're familiar with STD exams."

"Of course. A few crazy weekends in the Hamptons and we all get checked out."

"Well like I said, check it out if you're interested."

Their drinks came, and Paulie started a conversation with the attractive Israeli bartender in Hebrew.

Mick sipped his Jameson and sat down next to the pretty Russian doctor.

"Whatcha drinkin'? You want a drink or what?" he asked.

"*Stoh vie hiteetee?*"

"Say what?"

"I am sorry. I read charts, and it excites me," she said, in a very heavy accent.

Mick glanced at the pile of papers. They appeared to be medical records.

She covered them up with the white envelope as soon a she realized Mick was looking at them.

"I sorry. Medical records confidential. You must not look!"

"Yeah, I guess I am a little nosy being a lawyer and all."

"Vie advocate, da? I am sorry—I mean you are attorney, yes?"

"Yes, I'm a lawyer."

"Why lawyers not like US doctors? They make suing against them."

"No, I like doctors, especially pretty Russian ones. I work for a brokerage house downtown. I do mergers and acquisitions."

"What that?"

"My company buys and sells businesses. You might say I am a big capitalist."

"Capitalism, now good in Russia."

"Capitalism good everywhere."

"I must learn about capitalism to be good American doctor, yes?"

"Yes, all doctors in America are capitalist. They make good money"

"This I know."

"I am sorry. My name is Mick Ryan, and yours?"

"I am called Lala. It mean 'dolly' in Russian."

"Well, hello, Dolly."

Mick gave her a cheesy grin.

The young Russian doctor looked at him, puzzled.

"I'm sorry. It's a famous American musical. You know." Mick began to sing. "Hello Dolly, well hello Dolly.

It's so nice to be back where you belong. You're looking swell, Dolly, I can tell Dolly."

"You are very bad singer, and as you say, right?"

"Yeah, right," Mick said with a tone of disgust in his voice.

"You mad cause I tell you bad singer?"

"Well it's not the nicest thing anyone has ever said to me. Hey, you need a drink."

"I not drink alcohol, but I like grapefruit drink. Okay?"

Mick motioned to the bartender who was in a conversation with Paulie.

"Give the doctor a grapefruit drink and I will take another Jameson. Make it a double, neat."

"You drink whiskey, yes?"

"Yeah, we Irish are famous for our whiskey drinking."

"Yes, I know. I can see on your nose you are a whiskey drinker."

"What!"

"Yes, in Russia the men your age have red noses too," the young doctor said causally.

"Well in America, we usually don't talk about stuff like that."

"Same thing happen to Russian men. At forty they stop having sex and only want vodka."

"Well, when it comes to whiskey or pussy, I think I am an equal opportunity type of guy, if you know what I mean."

"No, I not understand what you mean."

"I mean I like girls and booze the same."

"Drink will take over, not careful."

"I know my limits."

The whiskey and the grapefruit juice arrived, and the young bartender immediately returned to Paulie, reengaging their conversation.

"Your friend likes that zhida girl, yes?"

"What is a zhida?"

"I sorry I should not use such word. It how you say Russian slang for female Jew?"

"In America we call them Japs—Jewish American Princesses."

"Are they part of royalty?"

"No, they just think they are."

The young Russian doctor checked her watch. "I come to this bar to catch men. I like sex and try every day to have it. You like sex, yes?"

Mick paused before he answered. He couldn't come up with a flip answer. He wanted this little Russian; he didn't need to lose her to a wise-ass remark.

"Yes, I like sex, believe it or not. I like you. You're smart and sexy. Good combination."

"How big you hooey? I sorry, I mean you dick."

"Wow, you really get to the point!"

Mick held up his right hand and drew a line with his left hand from the top of his wrist to the top of his middle finger.

"About that big."

"Normal."

The young Russian turned over his wrist and placed her finger three inches below the top of his wrist. She ran her index finger from that point to the tip of his middle finger.

"Russian men that big." She looked him in the eyes and smiled.

"Well what can I say?"

For the second time she checked her watch. "Are you interested in fucking me?" she asked.

"Of course."

"I need your name, real name, take it from driver license and phone number. You call and maybe come tomorrow, here?"

"What's your rush today?"

"How you Americans put it. I have fuck date at six."
The young doctor retrieved a pen from her purse and asked

Mick to write down his name and phone number. He began to write, and she said, "I need to see driver's license, please."

The young doctor labored to study the plastic card as Mick printed his name and address off of his New York State driver's license.

Mick asked for his driver license back. She examined it again with the thoroughness of an Eastern European border guard and handed it back to him.

"Call you tomorrow and maybe we set fuck date. Yes?"

"Yes, fuck date!" Mick repeated.

The Russian doctor slid off the stool. Mick observed every motion, feeling the anticipation in his crotch.

He returned to Paulie who was still chatting up the young Israeli.

Mick interrupted with, "Fuck, is she hot! Maybe tomorrow. She'll call."

"Good," said Paulie, returning to his conversation with the bartender.

"When did you start speaking heebie geebie?"

"I began studying Hebrew when I converted after college. I become fairly fluent over the past several years and speak it every chance I get."

"Speaking of Hebs, ya here the one about the Catholic priest and the rabbi walking past a school yard and the priest says to the rabbi, 'Wanna screw some kids and the rabbi replies, 'Out of what?'"

Both the bartender and Paulie were silent.

The bartender spoke first. "That's terrible that you mixed pedophilia with the myth that Jewish people have a need to take money unjustly for others."

"Christ, don't you people have any humor?"

The woman looked directly at Mick and addressed him in Hebrew.

"Not bad, Mick. Not bad at all. You managed to score twice today. Once with the Russian, now with barkeep."

"What the hell did she say?" demanded Mick after the bartender finished and stood behind the bar, staring intently at Mick.

"Well, loosely translated, I'm still working on some of the slang, she said, if your dick is a big as your mouth, she wants to fuck you, too."

"Very funny. I'd show her, but I understand Jews can't eat pork. That's the only thing I'd let her do to me."

"I know English, so Paul does not have to tell me, and I do eat pork."

"Truce!" said Paulie.

"I had a whole new repertoire of jokes, but I'll save them for an appreciative audience." Mick paused and then began again. "I gotta tell this one it's so good and very timely. I swear, if you think it's offensive I'll give a hundred bucks to the united Jewish whatever."

"Okay! Okay!"

"Here you go. A Catholic priest, Jewish rabbi, Protestant minister, Buddhist monk, and Muslim imam walk into a bar. The bartender says, 'What is this, some sort of joke?'"

Both the bartender and Paulie laughed.

"Mick, thanks for keeping it straight," Paulie said.

"Good, joke," the bartender said, "but you are still an asshole."

"Hey, Paulie, how do you say 'bitch' in Hebbie?"

"Stop now! Stop now!" Paulie said.

"I can't leave this lovely lady without an Irish Blessing. This is for both of you. 'May all of your children be healthy, wealthy, and wise and all marry Palestinians.'"

At work the next day, every few minutes Mick checked his cell phone to see if he had a message from the Russian doctor. With the market in the toilet, he needed to get laid. Work was playing out like a death watch with people being axed every day. He had a few bucks in the bank, but the thought of job loss constantly weighed on his mind.

He lived in Brooklyn Heights, in a great apartment even by New York standards. He had a few girlfriends. A couple of serious ones. The thought of marriage and kids was not even a blip on his radar.

His own mother and father had been older parents. His mother had been in her early forties when he was born and his dad in his fifties. They'd died a few years back, within a few months of each other. They lived in the same house in Floral Park, Long Island, for more than forty years. Good Catholics, very good parents. Their deaths still bothered Mick.

His childhood friend, Paulie, was one of the last reminders of his youth. The two of them had been inseperable as kids but took different paths after high school. Catholic school all the way for Mick. He stayed at Fordham University for both undergraduate and his MBA. He went to Loyola Law School.

Picked up by a Wall Street company right out of school, he had stayed with the same firm ever since.

His parents could never understand the culture of downtown Manhattan. His mother bought him a very expensive tie one Christmas. She wanted him to be the best dressed in his office. He never explained the hierarchy that existed on Wall Street. Be humble. Don't try to out-shine those above you and, for God sakes, never out-dress the boss.

He worked with a lot of Jews and kept his humor to himself. Many of the younger Jewish employees in his office wore yarmulkes, but they kept to their own. Not too many Irish Micks on the Street.

Paulie's conversion to Judaism came as a shock to Mick. Comfortable with his Catholic faith, Mick still went to mass often. Occasionally, he'd attend his parent's old church in Brooklyn. Holy Cross held dear memories that both his mother and father shared with him.

His Catholic education had been a combination of lay people and the last of the old Polish nuns of Saint Hedwig's in Floral Park. God bless them, they were crazy as hell but made him learn. His parents sent him to a private Catholic Jesuit boy's school in the city for high school. The tuition was high, but they wanted their boy to have the best. Unlike Paulie, he had no student loans to pay off. His parents took care of it.

Now, on the cusp of thirty, Mick was still in search of a life, any life.

Suddenly, his cell phone rang. "This is Lala. Can you see me today?"

"Well, hello Dolly."

"Please not sing again, please."

"No singing, promise."

I can meet you at Doc's Bar. Maybe little after five."

"I can do five"

"You be horny, yes?"

"Oh yes. I be horny."

He hung up. His first thought was to call Paulie and thank him for the hook-up with the Russian girl. He began to thumb in Paulie's' cell phone number then stopped.

Over the last few years, he and his friend had grown apart. As a resident at City Hospital, Paulie worked long hours and slept in his spare time. Mick's nine-to-five life didn't fit in.

Mick tried to humor Paulie with his jokes. But Paulie's responses to his humor, especially his jokes about Jews, were often met with sighs and shakes of his head. Paulie, more often than not, greeted his friend with small talk consisting of the weather or the Yankees.

Mick asked Paulie once how he could give up Christ. His response: "I never gave up Christ. He gave me up." They never talked about their religious differences again, other than his Jewish jokes—which Mick felt funny and worth passing on.

He decided he'd call Paulie after the event with the Russian girl. Just another piece of ass, a nice piece, but just the same, a piece of ass.

Mick took off work a few minutes early. He wanted to beat the traffic before it invaded up town. But most of all he wanted to make sure he wasn't late for his meeting with the young doctor.

As he entered Doc's he waved at the young hostess in the nurse's uniform and just said, "Bar."

His thought was that after he finished with the young Russian doctor, he'd make sure to come back and try his luck with the pretty nurse hostess.

Greeted by the same young Israeli bartender of the day before, he offered his paltry attempt at Hebrew. "Shlam," he said.

"Shlam is Arabic. We say shalom. What you want?" she said coldly.

"Give me two grapefruit drinks, no ice," he replied.

She left the bar, and he heard a barely audible "Prick" from the Israeli girl.

The young Russian doctor appeared about five minutes later, sliding next to him on the bar stool.

"You early, I see!"

"Yes, I wanted to make sure I didn't miss you. I took the liberty of ordering two grapefruit drinks."

"I need to wait a few minutes for package—then we go to my apartment."

She handed him a piece of paper with an address on East 40th.

"Why you not drink whiskey, like yesterday?"

"I just wanted to be my best for you, that's all."

"Best?"

"Yeah, yesterday you mentioned that Russian men who drink too much are a bunch a limp dicks. So I thought I'd do it cold sober."

"What you mean limp dicks?"

Mick held up his index finger, pointed toward the young woman's face, and gradually loosened his finger until it was a ninety-degree angle.

"Yes. I know limp dick."

They were interrupted by the same young man in the leather coat from the day before. He placed a large envelope on the counter and walked away without conversation.

"I have business," she said. "I go ahead to my apartment. Give me fifteen minutes. You not be disappointed, promise."

Mick sipped the rest of his drink and watched the bar clock. The Israeli came to him twice to ask if he needed anything. He wanted to order a double Jameson but didn't want to face the young Russian with booze on his breath; plus, the night before he'd spent a fair amount of time in front of his bathroom mirror studying the small veins in his nose.

His mother referred to it as the "map of Ireland" that all Irish men developed despite their level of booze consumption.

His father had it. He was a one-Tom-Collins-a-night guy.

He pledged to himself he would talk to Paulie about getting a referral to a dermatologist to get a laser zap. He'd read something about it in *Men's Health* magazine, thought it was time he got something done.

The Russian woman's apartment was only a few blocks from the bar. He gave himself a few minutes to get there lest he be too early, too anxious.

He knew the neighborhood well. His father had taken him for walks there when he was a kid. Block by block he retraced his family's various living quarters on the East Side of Manhattan. When his father was a boy, the family church was St. Andrew's on East Forty-Third. Once the parish of choice for many of the East Side Irish, it now served as a homeless shelter with a limited mass schedule.

Mick wanted to clear his head of any thoughts of St. Andrew's. Sex and church weren't to be mixed, despite the recent revelation of the parish priest and his exploits with children.

He was about a half block from the address now, between Third and Second Avenues.

He examined the building as he walked toward it. A typical East Side apartment building built in the late eighties or early nineties with light red brick and plenty of glass.

He glanced across the street at the old fire station next to the three-story tenement. He remembered what his father had told him when he was a child.

"Son, study these buildings, cause when you're a man, they'll be gone. Some rich Jews will be collecting rent for other rich Jews in big apartment buildings."

Mick smiled to himself. His mother always corrected him when he made anti-Semitic remarks. His dad would always smile back with a wink.

The building entrance was set back from the street about fifty feet. In front of the revolving chrome and glass door, stood a large doorman.

As Mick approached the door, the doorman stepped forward. Looking down on Mick he asked, in a heavily accented voice, "How may I help you?"

This place, as his father would say, was pretty swanky.

He didn't want to say he was here to see Lala, but that was all the name he needed to get in.

The doorman repeated, "How, I help you, please?"

Mick cleared his throat. "I'm here to see a friend. She's a Russian doc and her name is Lala."

The doorman stared at him. He had an urge to flee, to get back to the bar and down several well-deserved shots of Jameson.

The doorman looked up and down the street as if he were searching for someone before he said, "Yes, doctor is waiting for you."

Once inside, Mick walked toward the concierge desk.

The man looked up from his computer screen. "Yes?"

"I'm here to see the Russian doctor, Lala."

The clerk looked at the doorman.

Mick gazed over for a moment. He followed the clerk's eyes toward the doorman, observed his nod to the man behind the counter, an affirmative yes.

"Yes, the doctor is expecting you. She is in twenty-seven I. Exit the elevator and make a left, second door down."

As Mick entered the elevator, the thought crossed his mind that the good doctor must receive a lot of guests. Mick's nut sack suddenly hitched up a few notches toward his belly.

Things didn't add up. Russian immigrant doctor, here to pass American medical boards, lives in a place where the rent is at least four grand a month.

Mick hesitated before he hit the twenty-seven on the elevator keypad.

Sex was supposed to be exciting. He was excited in the wrong way. His excitement was turning to alarm, his fear ratcheting up with every floor he passed.

His suspicions were allayed once he thought of his friend Paulie. Paulie knew the setup, had encouraged him to get to know the doctor.

With that in mind, he exited the elevator and walked down the hall until he found himself in front of twenty-seven I. He drew back his hand to knock. Before he touched the door it opened. The young Russian doctor stared at him.

"I hear elevator. Very expensive building but the walls are not thick."

She stepped back to let Mick in.

Mick viewed the apartment with a sense of relief. A studio—he estimated the rent at about twenty-five hundred a month rather than his first estimate of a full apartment at four thousand.

His relief was short-lived as he saw the sparsely furnished space. It reminded him of a waiting room in a doctor's office. Something else caught his eye—a hospital gurney.

He managed to say, "What's with the funny bed?"

The doctor giggled. "I think you Americans call it fetish. I can only fuck on hospital bed. Something I learned in medical school. I like to be fucked on these type beds."

Mick felt mild relief in his groin as the young doctor snickered.

"Please take clothes off. I want you naked. Maybe your friend explains that I cannot use condom. I take blood sample then we can fuck. Right?"

"Right." Mick took off his suit jacket, loosened his tie.

"You not afraid of needle? Yes?"

Mick looked at the young doctor and the smile on her face.

He wanted her, but he also wanted to get out of this place as soon as he did her.

She must have sensed his anxiety. She stepped back and pulled off the top of her green scrubs.

The whiteness of her skin, her perfectly symmetrical yet tiny titties brought reassurance to his tense body.

"You like little boobies, yes?"

"Oh, yes!" Mick groaned as he reached out, caressing her small breasts.

She pulled away. "Business first, as you say. I must test blood before we fuck."

Mick began to take the rest of his clothes off as the semi-naked doctor turned her back and arranged a simple tourniquet, syringe, and needle on the gurney.

"Hey, you know I am really clean. No sex without a rubber and all that."

"I know you okay, but as a doctor I cannot take any chances. Simple blood test and we can as you say 'Get at it.'" The young doctor smiled and motioned Mick to sit on the gurney.

"Just a little prick and then we can do blood work," she said.

"Hey, watch it with that 'little prick' stuff," Mick mockingly scolded.

She looked puzzled. "You make joke, yes?"

"I tried."

The doctor applied the rubber tourniquet to Mick's left arm.

"Make fist, please."

He made a fist, pumped his hand.

"You not need to do that," the doctor said quietly.

"Sorry," said Mick. "When I was an undergrad our fraternity gave blood every quarter to the Red Cross. We used to have races on who could fill the bag the quickest. So every time I have to give blood I start pumping my hand."

The doctor gave Mick a strange look.

"It's an American thing."

She drew the vial of blood.

"Please, I need a few minutes to test blood. You lie down and rest."

The lawyer laid back on the gurney. Naked, relaxed, he fantasized about the story he would tell Paulie. Who the fuck's gonna believe it?

He heard movement in the kitchen. The clink of glasses like test tubes in high school class.

Mick grew restless. Always hyperactive, any sort of silence or nothingness for the shortest periods drove him nuts. He scanned the room. Nothing much—a simple white box of a room with some plastic chair and end tables.

What type of whack job could live in a place like this? On the heat register across the room in front of the window lay a white envelope. It was identical to the one the doctor had received earlier from the black leather-coated courier at Doc's Bar.

Mick slid surreptitiously from the gurney, padded over to the window, glanced in the galley kitchen, and made sure the coast was clear as he examined the folder.

The glued seal was broken. Mick peeled back the flap and fished out a small stack of Xerox copies.

The first thing he saw was his name on a medical form. He recognized it as being from his last physical. He flipped through the pages, realizing someone had compiled his complete medical history in twenty-some pages.

"What the fuck is this shit?"

"Not, what the fuck," the Russian doctor said. "You one who fucked."

He felt a sting in his left butt check as the needle hit his sciatic nerve. He gripped his left side. His last thought, his father walking with him down Fortieth Street twenty years before.

The buzz of the surgical saw stopped, the pink mist dusted over the white chest it had cut through. The surgeon grabbed the man's flabby breast muscle and pulled, creating a sucking sound. He placed the muscle and rib bones on the man's stomach.

The team looked down at the beating heart.

"Well, I'll be goddamn, the son of a bitch had a heart after all."

The young Russian doctor giggled, and the Israeli major pinched his butt cheek and winked.

"Schlepperchov, keep your jokes to yourself. We have kidneys and a liver to extract next. All of you keep your composure," scolded the old Russian doctor.

Paulie's only thought: three more of these and my medical school loans will be paid off!

The Mediterranean

Mayor Bloomberg warned people to stay home on every channel of the TV. The next few days were forecasted to be the coldest on record in the tri-state area. Vinny drove up Second Avenue. To his surprise, the street was virtually deserted.

New Yorkers prided themselves on toughness, but there's tough and then there's crazy.

Vinny considered himself a little of both.

He met with a man to discuss a development in Long Island City. The guy sounded legit; the project looked good on paper as far as finances and connections, both at the city and borough level.

The past several years, most of Vinny De Palma's dealings were above board. A few minor issues existed with offshore accounts and such. His interest in the project came from his desire to put the offshore money to work. Scrub money clean, the name of the game.

Vinny's money men assured him that after the offshore money was laundered and put to use he'd be as clean as the pope. Not a single dollar could be traced to him or his operations.

Post-Gotti New York was a different place. None of the old families existed—either because the feds busted them or God called home some of his more infamous mafiosos.

Vinny stepped into a small alcove at his favorite restaurant. The waiter-bartender greeted him. "The kitchen is closed. We're only serving drinks."

Vinny recognized the small Italian waiter behind the bar. He loved the little restaurant but possessed a real aversion to the waiter.

He was a semi-regular at the restaurant. Besides his mother's restaurant in Brooklyn, Vinny frequented this little joint more than any other. His favorite dish, the raviolis with the vodka reduction sauce. Phenomenal! The little wop behind the bar sucked the pleasure out of Vinny's dining experience right off with his kitchen's-closed bullshit.

Vinny hung up his coat, white scarf, and gloves and seated himself on a bar chair.

The skinny waiter spoke up. "Someone's sitting there."

Vinny, ready to blow on this guy, let his rage escape slowly with a deep breath. Defused a bit, he spoke through a clamped jaw. "What the fuck are you talkin' about?"

"I think he's talking about me," said a slightly accented voice from behind him.

Vinny turned toward the voice.

It belonged to a leggie blonde.

For his friends and anyone else who would listen to him, this is how Vinny would describe the woman:

She wore one of those white silky-type blouses. Underneath, braless, just one of those cami things. Her nipples kinda played peek-a-boo under her blouse. Her black leather skirt, halfway up her thigh with a slit to reveal a little extra. When she sat down, the skirt hiked up far enough to see her garter belt and the tops of her stockings. It wasn't long before I figured out she didn't wear panties.

She had natural blonde hair to her shoulders. Perfect teeth, juicy lips, not too small not too big, just nice.

Without a doubt, the most beautiful lady I'd ever met.

"Hey, I wasn't tryin' to cop your seat. I just figured no one but me and the guy I'm supposed to meet would be crazy enough to be out in this stuff."

"Please, have a seat," the tall blonde said.

"Sure, sure," replied Vinny.

Vinny got settled and waved the bartender over.

"Give me a Chianti and give the lady whatever she's having."

"Please, I cannot accept," the blonde said.

"A guy tried to steal ya chair. It's the least I can do."

"Okay, but only one and you must let me buy the next round."

She turned to the bartender. "Chianti."

Vinny planned to offer a protest but held back. "I'm pretty good with accents, but for some reason I can't place yours."

The tall blonde flipped her head back, revealing her stunning smile. "Oh, yes! My accent! It always seems to get me into trouble. But believe it or not I am an American. Born in New York but raised in Europe. My father was an art appraiser. So my life as a child was spent in a series of private European schools."

"Interesting story. I don't think I got out of Brooklyn until I was twenty-one."

They both laughed.

"So what brings you out tonight?" asked the blonde.

"I'm supposed to meet some guy about a real estate deal. This weather may be a deal breaker."

"So you are a real estate man!"

"Kinda sorta," said Vinny.

"Kinda?"

Vinny almost reached for a business card. Too pushy.

"I do some properties, got some retail, a few restaurants, apartments, and an import/export company."

"You are quite the entrepreneur, yes."

"Yeah, I guess you can say that."

"You and Donald Trump." The lady smiled playfully.

"I and the Donald have very little in common. I pay my bills, stay out of bankruptcy courts."

"I take it you and Mr. Trump doesn't get long."

"Put it this way. We try to avoid each other's company."

"Are you insulted?"

"By you, never. By the way, what are you into?"

"Like my father, I am into art."

"You an artist?"

"Oh no, far from it. I am what you may call a fine art broker."

"Never heard of one."

"Let me give you an example. Someone has some financial problems or there is an impending death in the family. They call me and I very quietly dispose of art for them. I beat the tax man in both cases."

"I bet the IRS would like to get a hold of your client list."

"I am sure, but I provide a very worthwhile service to my clients."

The bartender reappeared and asked if the couple wanted another round.

"Yes, please," she said.

She turned to Vinny. "Remember, I am paying for this round."

"Of course."

The bartender returned with fresh glasses of Chianti.

"I am dying for a cigarette," she said.

"I tell you what, you step outside and you'll die in this weather."

"This smoking ban thing is so uncivilized."

"Not being a smoker and all, except for a cigar now and then, I can't sympathize."

Vinny noticed the coldness that overcame his beautiful companion.

"But being the New York gentleman that I am, I think I can fix things for you."

"Fix?"

Vinny raised his hand, and the bartender approached him.

"I bet ya fifty bucks this place don't got an ashtray."

The bartender reached under the bar, producing a white ceramic ashtray with The Mediterranean's name and logo.

Vinny reached into his wallet and placed a fifty dollar bill on the bar top.

"I lose!" Vinny offered in a mock defeat.

"Please, you did not have to do this."

"Oh, yes I do. How could I let a beautiful woman like you go outside? I mean, what the hell, I might never see you again."

The lady reached into a cigarette box with the name "Milano" printed in blue letters on a white background.

Vinny reached for the book of matches that accompanied the ashtray.

He struck the match, brought it towards the lady's face. With the light of the match he got a closer look at her faultless skin. He also noticed she wore no makeup.

She took a long drag of her cigarette, blew the smoke out through slightly pursed lips, and sent a plume of white smoke across the bar.

Smoke reached the waiter at the end of the bar. He fanned his face, rolled his eyes, and left the area for the first table behind the bar. He took his copy of the New York Daily News with him.

Vinny's senses went wild. He breathed in the aroma of the cigarette. It was some kind of aromatic. He hated cigarette smoke, but this was different. The exotic smell caused his sense of smell to kick into overdrive. He could swear he smelled the leather from the lady's skirt and, more importantly, her body.

"Two questions," Vinny started.

"Mister, after getting me a cigarette, an ashtray, ask me any dark secrets you wish."

Known for his smartass remarks, Vinny's suave ways worked well on Brooklyn girls, but this one was in a whole new league.

"Nothing dark or secret, but I can't help notice you're smoking a cigarette that I've never heard of and you're not inhaling."

The blonde flipped her head back and laughed.

"Believe it or not, you have gotten into some very dark secrets by asking those questions."

"Hey, hey, I didn't mean...I mean, I didn't mean to get personal or anything," he stuttered.

"No, you're not getting personal, and I love the broken English that people from Brooklyn speak so, please, no need for grammar corrections."

Vinny, a multi-millionaire, loved being a power broker in New York. He resented his eighth-grade education at Holy Cross Grammar School in Brooklyn, thanks to his run-in with the nuns, the law, and the New York State Juvenile Justice system.

The blonde noticed his mood change.

"Oh I am so sorry. I have offended you, yes?"

"No, you have not offended me. You're right. I have a limited education and sometimes the obvious pokes through when I get, let's say, animated."

"Do I animate you?"

"Yes, but in a very good way."

They both laughed.

"Most men think I intimidate them."

"Being intimidated, no that's not my style." Vinny's bravado came back into his voice.

He motioned to the waiter. The skinny man made an exaggerated effort to fold his newspaper and make his way to the back bar.

"Hey, buddy, I notice you're having a real busy night. So why don't you leave the bottle. While you're at it, crack open another and leave it at the bar."

The waiter retrieved the open bottle and reached for another bottle of Chianti without a word.

"Where were we?" Vinny asked. "Oh, yeah. The dark side of your cigarette smoking."

"I can't believe I brought it out. It must be the wine's effect on me."

The waiter placed a newly opened bottle on the bar, refilled both glasses, and quickly retreated to his table and his Daily News.

"Let me answer your question first. Milanos are a private brand of cigarettes made in Milano, Italy, of course. They have very little tobacco, many exotic spices and herbs—thus those unusual smells."

"And the not inhaling?"

"That is the dark side," giggled the lady.

"How could anyone as lovely as you have a dark side?"

"My parents placed me in a boarding school in Berne, Switzerland, when I was thirteen years old. It was the equivalent of your high schools. My French teacher was a young Parisian man who took a year off of his studies to teach. Oh, my God, I thought he was the sexiest man I had ever seen. All the girls in our school were in love with him.

"We had an informal contest as to which of us he would choose as a lover."

"Wait a second—you where how old?" Vinny interrupted.

"I was thirteen, maybe fourteen."

"I'm sorry. I'll try not to interrupt again."

"Oh, please interrupt, it is only boring history. So anyhow, as you American's say, the contest was which of us girls could claim him as our lover. You have to understand, at the time I was a very skinny little girl. I mean no ass or breast, nothing. I was competing against some very mature girls who had experience with sex."

"Experienced at fourteen!"

The waiter blinked up at the couple and quickly returned to his paper.

"Oh, monsieur, this was in Europe, remember."

"Yeah, okay."

"Like I mentioned, I was out of my league, so to speak, with many of my classmates. So I had to devise a plan if I were to win over the Frenchman. For several days I followed him after school to his rooming house. He lived in a pathetic little garret on the third floor. On the third day I raced from the school and beat him to his rooming house.

"I was naked on his cot when he opened the door. He looked both shocked and excited when he discovered me.

"He crossed the small room with only two steps and was seated next to me on his smelly little cot.

"He said, 'Why are you here? I can get fired from my position at your academy and arrested by the authorities.'

"I assured him that I would never reveal him as my lover.

"He paced the small room, took a cigarette from his pants pocket, and sat on the cot again.

"'Do you smoke?' he asked me.

"'Of course,' I replied.

"It was a lie. I never smoked, but here I was a little girl with no breast and small patch of hair on my little puss, so what was I to say?

"I took his hand and took a puff of his cigarette and immediately blow out the smoke."

"Good for you, you don't inhale. Cigarettes will ruin your beautiful skin." Vinny offered up his fatherly advice.

"I took the good advice from my teacher and have never inhaled."

The blonde took another drag off her cigarette and smiled.

A moment passed before Vinny asked the inevitable question.

"And so, what happened?"

"Happened?"

"Yeah, happened?"

"He took off his clothes and sat next to me. He started that bullshit the French are known for, telling me how beautiful I was and how wonderful it would be. He grew aroused. I soon realized all the talk about Frenchman must be true. His private grew to the size of a ruler."

"A ruler?"

"Yes, what American would call a good foot?" She made a motion with her hands that approximated twelve inches.

The blonde waited for Vinny's response.

He drained his glass in anticipation.

"And?"

"He explored my body with his hands while he kissed my neck and small breasts. He was mumbling in French, which, at the time, I was not fully fluent in. He finally asked how many lovers I'd had. I whispered that he was the first. He jumped from the bed and began cursing that he was not a child molester and that I must leave.

"He reached for his pants pocket and took out another cigarette. His pocket watch fell on the bed. And I knew I had a plan."

"A plan?"

"Oh, yes, let me continue, please. The young teacher began each class by dramatically reaching into his pants pocket and taking out an old gold pocket watch. He would announce, 'Ladies, the next hour is mine!'

"I realized if I took his watch it would be proof that I was with the teacher and the contest would be mine, so to speak. The next day French class began, as usual.

"The young teacher stood before us and reached for his pocket as was his habit. The watch was not there. He began to mumble and turned his back to the class and began writing French verbs on the blackboard. I walked up to his desk with his watch and placed it on his desk. I retreated to my desk as the class began to giggle. He turned to chastise the class when he noticed the watch on his desk. He paused for a moment and began weeping and covered his face with his hands.

"He dismissed class and resigned that day. Our head mistress taught our French class for the rest of the term."

She smiled and took a sip of wine.

"So what did you get for winning?"

She smiled and sipped her wine.

"I was the most popular girl in my grade and maybe the entire academy. An upper-level girl took me as her roommate and her lover."

"You were what?"

She smiled coyly again and took a long drag from her cigarette.

"Please, this place was an exclusive girls school. All the girls had their little romances. I may have had a dozen different girls by the time I finished my studies."

Vinny reached for his wine glass. The blonde gently stroked the top of his right arm and moved down to his wrist. She locked her thumb and index finger around his wrist and pulled his hand to her exposed thigh. She pulled his hand up her leg until she was sure Vinny could feel the end of her stockings and the beginning of her exposed legs.

Vinny exhaled.

"I thought men liked to hear about girls together, yes? Does my little story excite you?"

"I would have to be a eunuch for it not to excite me, and yeah, guys like that stuff."

"I have a lot of stories, if you have the time."

The lady reached for the bottle of Chianti and Vinny's hand landed gentle on top of hers.

"I have the time, but you gotta understand, us Italian guys have this thing about being gentlemen. So I hafta pour, if you don't mind."

"Please pour and keep it coming."

Vinny noticed a slight slur in her speech.

In the short time they chatted at the bar they'd consumed about four glasses of wine between them. He prided himself on his high alcohol tolerance but realized he'd skipped lunch, and he looked forward to a nice plate of raviolis with his new business partner. He was famished.

Vinny eyed the waiter.

"Hey, waiter, what's the chance of gettin' a couple of plates of raviolis here?"

Without looking up from his paper, the waiter said, "Like I said, the kitchen is closed."

Vinny excused himself and approached the punk. The skinny man flinched when he realized Vinny was standing over his table.

"Easy, guy. I just need some food. Nothin' special. Just a couple of plates of raviolis, and I'll do the cooking."

Before the waiter could protest, a hundred dollar bill fell on the table top.

"Cook away."

Vinny returned to the bar as the lady poured them both another glass of wine.

"Hungry?" he asked.

"I know it is very unladylike to mention it, but I am fucking starving."

"How about a lesson in Italian cooking?"

"Do I get to taste anything else Italian?"

"We can work on it!"

Vinny escorted the lady toward the back of the restaurant to the kitchen. He noticed she had a slight sway to her gait.

Vinny pushed open the double-hinged kitchen doors. A prep area lamp was on and through instinct he reached behind the door to feel for an overhead. He hit one switch and half a bank of florescent lights flicked on. He hit the second switch, and the kitchen was aglow in white light.

The young blonde covered her eyes.

"Wow, kill some lights please."

"What, you some kinda vampire or what?"

"I show you vampire if you can get me some fresh garlic, olive oil, and balsamic."

Vinny opened the stainless steel doors to the refrigerator.

"Let me get some sauce and raviolis out first."

Vinny looked over the shelves and spotted the uncut tray of fresh raviolis. He reached in and pulled out a rack to show the tall blond.

"How hungry?"

She surveyed the rack and replied, "Fucking hungry."

Vinny placed the raviolis on the prep table and reached for another.

With his back to the lady he heard her say, "When I said I was fucking hungry, why did you think I meant food?"

"No self-respecting Italian would let a lady make love on an empty stomach. But if you want an appetizer this water will take about ten to boil and—"

Before he completed his sentence, her blond hair was in his face and her lips were on his.

He could taste her scented cigarette, the Chianti on her sweet breath. Her lips were full and moist. She slowly pulled her lips back and traced over his lip line with her wet tongue.

He opened his mouth, and her tongue entered, searching with a teasing tickle motion. His hand reached up and cupped her breasts—firm, not hard, definitely real.

She broke off first.

"My turn to razzle dazzle. You get on the stove and let me do the bread."

"Let me help you find some of the stuff," said Vinny.

"Look, spaghetti boy, do you think you are the only one who knows their way around a kitchen?"

"Deal." Vinny backed off.

The prep area soon became a proving ground as to who could get their portion of the meal to the plate first.

Vinny sniffed the containers of sauces to make sure he selected the vodka reduction sauce.

The blonde looked through drawers and retrieved a small paring knife and garlic press, surveying each as if they were battle tools.

Vinny filled the small pan with water.

The lady selected two cloves of garlic from the overhead basket.

Vinny lit the stove and added a pinch of sea salt to the water and a splash of olive oil.

She peeled and sliced the garlic.

He heated the vodka sauce in a pan over a slow fire.

The garlic was pungent as it emerged through a small steel hand press, tiny chunks falling onto a white dinner plate. The garlic joined with the olive oil and balsamic vinegar. A loaf of Italian bread steamed on the prep table, and she quickly sliced it into thick pieces. The concoction she topped with a squeeze from a lemon and then she spread the oily paste spread over the bread.

She took a piece of the treated bread and faced Vinny.

"Bite," she commanded.

Vinny took a large bite of the bread. The flavor sat on his tongue for a moment before it exploded to his senses.

"Holy shit, what did you do to that bread? It's great!"

"Garlic is the ultimate aphrodisiac," she purred.

Vinny reached for a lemon slice and rubbed her fingers.

"Lemons take away the garlic smell," he explained.

"I think I have something better."

She stepped back from Vinny, pulled open her leather slit skirt, and revealed a batch of light blonde hairs between her legs. She held open her shirt with her left hand while her right hand massaged her pussy. Three fingers disappeared inside her.

Her skirt dropped and she stepped towards Vinny. Their bodies touched as she brought her right hand up to his face. He smelled the garlic and lemon, but mostly he smelled her sweet musk on her fingers.

He embraced her tightly, squeezing her against his body, feeling her nakedness.

She whispered in his ear, "Let me get the Chianti and we'll do this right."

Vinny watched her walk from the kitchen. His attention turned to the pot of water and the trays of uncooked raviolis. He added a pinch of salt and a splash of olive oil to the water and waited.

A few minutes passed. He took a nip of the lady's garlic bread. This time the bread tasted slightly bitter as it hit his taste buds.

The water bubbled on the rim of the pot. Something his mother used to say about a watched pot came to mind. His mother wanted him to settle down with a good woman, have grandbabies for her. The blonde didn't appear to be the motherly type, but X-rated sex kitten for sure. He had plenty of fuck friends but no one to bring home to mom. This gal reeked of class and sophistication. From her conversation, she appeared pretty well off financially, so she wouldn't try to jockey for his money.

The water was at a full boil now. He broke up the tray of raviolis and placed them in the pot. Several minutes passed, more than enough time for the lady to get the bottle and be back.

Vinny pushed through the kitchen door and saw the waiter at his table, nose still in the Daily News. He quickly scanned the restaurant. No tall blonde.

Vinny addressed the waiter. "Is she in the restroom or what?"

"She left."

Vinny lost his temper and upended the table. The Daily News shot across the floor.

"What the fuck are you talkin' about?" Vinny hovered over the waiter now.

The little man, frightened, said, "Look, guy, the lady took her coat and went outside. I don't know if she went to smoke or what." The waiter's voice quivered.

"How long ago?" Vinny demanded.

"To be honest, maybe seven or eight minutes ago."

Vinny raced to the front door. The cold hit him as soon as he reached the first step up to the street. Mayor Bloomberg had successfully scared the hell out of New Yorkers with only a few cars traveling on Second Avenue.

The cold wind was too much for his cashmere sports coat. He retreated to the warmth of the restaurant. The waiter now stood behind the bar purposely. It created a barrier between himself and the angry Italian.

Vinny sensed the little guy's fear, realized he'd only get information from him if he remained calm.

The waiter stood defensively.

"Sorry for the outburst. I was just upset. You know, you think things are going well with a lady and she bolts on ya."

The waiter cleared his throat before he began to talk. "Look, all I know is the lady left the kitchen, came to the bar, grabbed her coat and the bottle of Chianti, and hit the street."

"Did she say anything?"

The waiter shook his head.

Vinny left the bar and drove the East Side for several hours with hopes he might find her.

He awoke the next morning exceptionally hard. His fingers rubbed his upper lips, the slight smell of garlic, lemon, and musk still there.

No dream after all.

In the shower he thought twice before he washed his face lest he scrub her scent away.

His calendar clear, he knew what he needed to do.

The drive into the city was met predictably with light traffic over the Brooklyn Bridge.

Radio weather said the arctic cold snap would last a few more days.

He parked on Fiftieth and walked around the corner to the restaurant. He wrestled with what he'd say to the owner of The Mediterranean. They were associates, not friends.

Vinny knew he had to tread lightly with his query into the mysterious blonde.

He entered the restaurant. The owner, Joey Messina, sat behind the bar.

"Vinny De Palma. Good morning. So what do I owe the pleasure?"

"Joey." A man's reputation in certain quarters of the city could be ruined by a loudmouth like Joey if he spoke crazy.

Vinny continued. "So Joey, I was here last night and I met this beautiful blonde in the bar. I was making time with her and all of a sudden, she fucking disappears."

A smile crossed Joey's face. "No shit, you fuckin' gaboon. You scared the shit out of my waiter. Little Tito is fuckin' afraid of his own shadow. He said you were completely dubots last night."

"No, not dubots. Maybe a little horny."

"Horny! The ways Tito described this woman, any man would give his grandmother's eyes for a sniff of her pussy."

"Yeah, you called it, Joey. She was one hot number. But I think it was the Chianti."

"Hot? She must be to get Vinny De Palma into my restaurant at eleven in the morning."

Vinny started to explain the reason for his early visit to the restaurant when Tito emerged from the kitchen doors. Visibly shaken by the sight of Vinny, he stopped in his tracks.

Both men noticed his reaction.

"For god's sake, Tito, come on over here. I know Vinny. He ain't no monster!"

The mousy waiter eased in behind the bar, huddling close to his boss.

"Look, Tito, sorry if I spooked you last night, but let's get to the facts. The lady was hot. She disappeared. I'm here to ask you and Joey if you ever seen her here before."

Joey spoke first. "The way you and Tito talk about her I'm sure if I had that lady in my place and had a chance I would have violated my marriage vows."

Joey and Vinny laughed. The waiter remained silent.

"I came in this morning to make amends with Tito." With that said, Vinny reached into his pocket, brandished a money clip, and laid a hundred dollar bill on the bar.

The slight waiter eagerly snatched the bill up and stuffed it into his apron.

Vinny and Joey engaged in small talk about weather and the economy then Vinny excused himself.

For the next few days Vinny called every contact he had about the possible identity of the tall blonde. He called curators at the Museum of Modern Art and the Guggenheim. He asked the same questions about a very attractive blonde art broker. No one had any information.

Not ready to give up, he called hotel concierge desks at the Plaza, Waldorf, and Four Seasons. Nothing.

He even called his accountant, asked if he knew of some art broker in town who sold estate art.

Every attempt to find his blonde obsession left Vinny empty-handed.

Every Sunday, since he was a boy, he and his mother had set time aside in the late afternoon for their family dinner.

The simple routine consisted of a single glass of Chianti, a small plate of antipasto, and a dish of Sunday gravy and rigatoni.

"So, Vincento, how you week go?" Momma asked in her Sicilian accent.

Vinny stared at his mother, who, in her early seventies, remained a very attractive lady with a slender body and silver hair. Her face glowed with smooth skin, soft laugh lines, and a gentle smile.

"Momma, things are good. Business is good."

"What about a woman in your life?"

"Momma, I know she is out there, promise."

The Home Bar

Deloris Dean woke at five a.m. Most mornings she spent a few minutes in bed mentally organizing her day. This morning, the last thing she wanted to do was to think. Today, she'd tell him he needed to get home to Missouri, to his family, get his ass back in school. Yes, today was the day.

Deloris was the sole proprietor of the Home Bar, located in the four corners area of Colorado in a shithole of a town called Rock Creek. Deloris had been there more than thirty-five years.

She had come out to Colorado with her husband. They hailed from a small Catskill mountain town—Round Top, New York. Tourism had dried up in the mid-sixties. Work for ranch hands pretty much dried up altogether.

Both Deloris and her husband, Gene, worked at assorted dude ranches in the Catskills. Both led city folks on trail rides. Life was easy until people stopped vacationing upstate.

A real horse ranch outside of Durango offered Gene a job as a foreman. The couple packed what they could fit in the back of their pick up and headed west.

Deloris hated Colorado. She missed the Catskills. She found the mountains of Colorado too pointed, cold, and distant. In her beloved Catskills she felt warm and loved.

Life was easier before they moved to Colorado. Here, Gene worked seven days a week at the ranch, and Deloris took a job in Rock Creek as a waitress in a bar and grill.

Things went well for the first three years in Colorado. Both worked hard and saved what they could to buy their home, a small three-bedroom ranch on the edge of town.

In the summer of 1969, hippies came. A bunch of California hippies set up camp about two hundred yards from Gene and Deloris's home. Peaceful, the group didn't drink or play loud music. Just smoked dope and occasionally strolled around stark naked.

Gene made friends with them, spent his spare time with them. He started to smoke a little dope and asked Deloris if she wanted to go over to their camp, smoke dope, and get naked. Disgusted, she declined.

One of the young girls wandered around the house. A pretty girl, about eighteen or so. Deloris noticed the girl wore no bra. Her full breasts bustled underneath her low-cut dresses.

The girl said she was from California, that she'd come to Colorado from Los Angles. She thought Colorado had God and good vibes. LA was full of poison.

One morning, Deloris noticed Gene's pickup at the hippy camp. Odd, she thought. He should be at work on the ranch.

Deloris was starting toward the camp when she watched Gene and the girl get into his pickup and drive toward their house. He pulled up to Deloris on the road. "There's this big music thing in New York at Woodstock. See you in a couple of weeks."

With that, Gene drove off down the road. She never saw him again.

She was stuck. The first few months were the worst. She considered suicide— After a few weeks, Deloris concluded Gene had abandoned her. Her first instinct was to sell the house and go back to New York. She contacted a real estate agent and explained as best she could the situation with Gene. The agent was sympathetic to her plight, but explained that since the home was in both their names. Deloris couldn't sell it without Gene's signature.

She developed her own mantra when she felt down: "No kids, no dogs, no sex, no problems."

This lasted thirty years until Sean showed up.

Since Deloris worked nights, she convinced herself she needed to keep busy by day until her night shift. Her ideas fluctuated between childcare or a day job. She went out on a limb and opened a barbecue stand in her front lawn. Slow at first, the business picked up when the Penny Lode Mine opened. The miners came by after their morning shift for smoky meat. After they worked twelve-hour shifts, the miners were in no condition to cook. They wanted to eat, clean up, go to bed, and do the whole thing over again the next day.

Generally a motley bunch, the miners desired more than food. Deloris sold beers under the counter without a liquor license. Business boomed until a sheriff's deputy stopped by to inform her she'd broken the law selling beer to the miners without a liquor license.

The deputy started to write her up a summons when she said, "Deputy, is there anyway we can settle this out of court?"

Deloris was pretty then. The deputy caught her drift and settled with a quick fuck.

So much for no kids, no dogs, no sex.

Afterward, the deputy did encourage her to get a liquor license.

She applied for one with the county commission. She was denied because she didn't have a physical structure from which to serve food and beverages. She reapplied with her home as the structure. Home Bar was born. It had cost Deloris only a week in bed with the county commissioner.

Deloris jokingly referred to her pussy as her silent partner. She'd never had much of an appetite for sex, but she discerned quickly that men, especially those in power, had an atrocious predilection for sex and younger women.

Men were attracted to Deloris when she was young. She ignored most of them, took a fleeting interest in others. She vowed never to have another Gene in her life.

As business grew, Deloris ran out of living space in her house. She bought a double-wide and parked it behind the bar. Financially she did well for herself. As the years passed and Deloris grew older, she seemed to wither inside and out. Her mantra changed. *Stop thinking about men and sex. Stop thinking about God. Stop thinking altogether.*

Her business success came with trial and error. She wanted to accommodate the miners and the different shifts they worked. She found her niche and monopolized the local bar-and-grill industry. She paid off the bus driver to use her lot for pick-ups and drop-offs for all shifts.

The mine owners complained to her when the employees showed up drunk for morning shifts. She changed her opening hours to evenings after the day shift ended. Deloris worked seven days a week sometimes eighteen hours a day. Bartenders came and went as well as waitresses. The one consistency of the Home Bar, Deloris.

Things changed when he showed up. A nineteen-year-old boy from Missouri and his mongrel dog aimed to change her life.

She didn't remember the exact day but she knew it was a very hot day in May. The temperature was close to a hundred degrees.

The boy walked into her deserted bar, announcing, "Lady, my name is Sean. I've worked my ass off in this heat all day. I'm only nineteen years old, but right now I would kill for a cold beer."

Deloris eyed the boy. He had a Southeast Missouri University t-shirt with a purple hat that read AK and an upside down V. Deloris later learned this was Sean's fraternity Alpha Kappa Lambda.

It was three o'clock in the afternoon. The miners wouldn't filter in for another four hours.

Deloris had her fair share of college and summer kids who tried to get served.

She'd tell them to get the hell out or she'd call the law.

She recalled saying, "Sonny, I don't serve kids here, but you really look like you need a beer. So this is what I'm gonna do. I'm gonna give you a Bud Light in a Coca Cola cup."

"Lady, I love you, and I swear to God I would drink it if it were recycled from a donkey's dick as long as it was beer and cold."

Deloris laughed as she opened the Bud Light and placed it before the boy. He drank the beer in one long gulp.

"Ma'am, not to be rude or crude, but I really could use another beer."

Sean pushed the empty toward Deloris. She popped another. He started to gulp again and slowed down to little slips. With the third beer, he nursed it and talked to the old lady behind the bar.

"Please, Sean, call me DeeDee. Everyone does. Smart-asses refer to me as Double-D's. People are cruel and nature the cruelest as you age."

"Okay, DeeDee, can I have a menu? I mean I'm really starved."

"Yeah, what can I get ya?"

The boy studied the menu. "Burger, fries, and salad, if you got it."

"Got it," she replied.

Deloris was turning toward the kitchen when she heard a loud bark followed by a howl.

"Oh, shit. It's Buddy, my dog. He needs a bowl of beer."

"You give your dog beer?"

"Only a little now and then. I don't want him to turn into a lush, you know."

The two laughed.

"I'll get you a bowl, but for god's sake, get him out of your truck. It must be a hundred degrees."

"You mean I can bring him in here?" Sean asked, surprised.

"What the hell? I've already broken one law today. What's another one?"

Sean returned Deloris's smile and retrieved a bowl out of his SUV.

His dog was panting on the floor of the air-conditioned bar when Deloris returned from the kitchen.

She greeted the dog. "What a pretty dog. What is he?"

"Please don't call him pretty. I think he's gay. I don't want to encourage him. Buddy is a pit bull-boxer mix."

"Oh, Sean, you have such a good humor about you."

"I'm Irish. I can't help it. Born with it, I guess."

"Irish, are you? My people are Irish too."

"You mean you're from Ireland?"

"No, no. I'm from upstate New York. My people, that is. My mum and dad are from Ireland. I grew up in a small town called East Durham, New York."

Deloris noticed Sean's eyes begin to tear up.

"Did I say something to offend you, Sean?"

Tears cascaded down Sean's cheeks. He buried his face in his hands.

Deloris came around the bar and tried to comfort the boy. She had not hugged a man or anyone for so long, but she reached out and patted the boy's shoulder.

"That's okay, boy. Go ahead and cry."

Sean pinched the bridge of his nose to gain his composure. He cleared his throat several times before he tried to speak again.

"You see, my father is from the Catskills too. When you said East Durham, well, it kinda brought back some very nice memories of family, travel, all that stuff." He wiped his eyes with the back of his hand.

"How long's it been since you seen your kin?"
"Oh boy!" His eyes looked up to the heavens for recall. "About a year. Left school after my freshman year, headed out here to God's country."

Deloris sensed the sarcasm in the young man's voice.

"I see you've fallen in love with the place too."

"Oh, don't get me wrong, it's an okay place, but I do miss home and friends and all." Sean welled up again.

"Know the feeling. Some days I miss my Catskill Mountains so much I damn near cry. I dream of them at night." Deloris felt a catch in her throat as she thought about home.

After Sean finished his lunch, he asked for another beer, and he gulped it down and left, but not before he thanked Deloris for her hospitality and kindness.

For the next few weeks Sean showed up with Buddy every day about three o'clock. They talked about home.

Sean had come out to Colorado with one of his high school buddies. They'd gotten jobs doing repair work for a company that kept summer and winter homes in repair for their owners. Sean's buddy lasted three months. The quiet and solitude proved too much for him.

Occasionally, Sean used the pay phone. She heard him shout into the receiver. Other times, he'd stay by the phone for five or ten minutes after his calls. When he returned to the bar she noticed his tears.

Deloris never asked about his phone calls. But she could tell who was on the other line by the tone of his voice. Girlfriends calmed him. Parents set him off.

After a month, Deloris asked Sean to move in to her spare room in the double-wide. He'd been doing some work around the bar and wouldn't accept money, so Deloris felt she should give him free board. He gladly accepted.

The daily procedures at the Home Bar hadn't deviated in many years. The Indians came in at the end of the month with their government checks, the miners every other Thursday evening. The locals came and went sporadically.

Sean tended bar every evening. He hauled the beer in from the back when the supply got low.

Often some of the miners got unruly and Sean stepped in to protect Deloris and her place. She insisted she could handle herself and that he stay out of it but she'd eventually acquiesce to Sean's care.

"Sean, these are not men, they're animals. They'd have little regret in sticking you with a knife and going back for another beer," she'd say like a mother hen.

The local girls seemed to notice Sean too. A couple of times a week they'd show up to play pool and make sure Sean noticed them. Once in a while, Sean took one back to his room in the double-wide.

Deloris gave some advice. "Sean boy, these girls are bar trash. They're good for a quick fuck or suck. But God knows one of them is gonna try and trap you and tell you she's having your baby. Can you imagine being trapped for the rest of your life?"

One morning Deloris got out of bed and headed to Sean's room and rapped on the door.

"Sean, come to the bar before you leave for work."

She heard Sean grunt.

She opened the Home Bar like any other day.

Her main concern was how Sean would take what she was going to offer.

Sean walked in the back door, Buddy trailing behind.

"Mornin', DeeDee."

"Mornin', Sean."

"So what's up? You need stuff done before I head out or what?"

"No, no work today." Deloris took a breath and said, "Sean, I'm closin' the Home Bar. New owners are takin' over next week."

"What?"

"It's time we both moved on," she said flatly.

"What do you mean, move on? I thought we were doing fine."

"Boy, I've spent over half my life in this hell hole. You being here, us working together, showed me there's something else out there."

"Where will you go?" His face started to pout.

"I'm going home, Sean. Home to New York and my Catskill Mountains."

"And me, what am I going to do?"

"You, well, Sean, you should think about getting back to school."

She could see the anger boil up in Sean's face. He paced in a large circle in front of the bar before he began to talk.

"How can I go home? I have nothing. I've been working for over a year. I get by. I probably don't have enough money to get gas for the trip."

"Sean, you're going home and going back to school."

At a full boil now, Sean shot back, "Did you not hear me? I can barely fill my gas tank and you're talking about school. That cost money. I'm broke."

Deloris reached in her apron pocket and pulled out a white envelope and placed it on the bar.

"There is close to twelve thousand dollars in that envelope. I want you to take it and get your ass back to school. Get the hell out of this shithole of a town."

"What? I can't take that. What will you do?" He looked confused.

"Sean, I've wasted my life here. I'm gonna move on. Never spent a penny. I didn't have too. Some say I'm a rich lady."

Sean walked behind the bar. He opened his arms to hug Deloris.

"No, Sean. Please, no hugs. If you start hugging me, I'll never let go."

Sean pulled her close and squeezed. Deloris let herself wrap her arms around him and inhale his sweetness.

"Thank you," Sean whispered in her ear.

She let a tear escape the corner of her eye then wiped it quickly away and let go.

"This is goodbye, Sean boy."

The Butt Crack Bar

Nancy Schwartz was a significant person in my life. She was my literary agent.

Nancy made sure my work was ready for publication. In her own crude way, she stated it very clearly when she said, "I am the Vaseline in your ass before the publishers get a chance to fuck you."

Nancy called me to her office on Second Avenue to review my second novel. She liked to work with new writers. To her, new writers were pliable, easily manipulated.

"The veterans are the real pains in the ass," she said. "A couple of books under their belts and they try to tell me how to do my job."

I never could tell if it was a warning or idle chatter. She wasn't much of a talker, so I took it as a warning.

My first novel, Visiting Brooklyn, was a moderate success. A few weeks on the *USA Today* and *New York Times* best-seller lists. Nancy worked on a movie deal and possible HBO series options.

For now, however, my second endeavor was the focus.

"We have to fight against the sophomore jinx," she said.

A myth shared by publishing houses and literary agents was that if a first time author had a best seller the first time out, the second effort was probably jinxed. To ward off the curse, Nancy asked me to do something a little different. "Don't come out with a sequel. Try to do something you're comfortable with."

I pitched the idea of doing a book about growing up with an Irish father and the characters I saw in bars.

"Okay. Then why not include characters you've viewed in your life and some wild drinking tales about 'bar whores' and such in a collection of short stories?" she suggested.

Yes, Nancy came up with the title. She now felt a deep kinship with my book and wanted to make sure "we" had another "baby together. After a few weeks, Deloris concluded Gene had abandoned her. Her first instinct was to sell the house and go back to New York. She contacted a real estate agent and explained as best she could the situation with Gene. The agent was sympathetic to her plight, but explained that since the home was in both their names Deloris couldn't sell it without Gene's signature."

Six months later, I was back in her office with some final drafts of eight different short stories for a collection "we" were going to call *Bar Whores*.

"Give me three weeks and get back," was all she offered.

Three weeks later, Nancy sat quietly, flipping through my manuscript reviewing her margin notes.

Besides being one of the ugliest people I've ever met, Nancy Schwartz had no discernable affect. She showed virtually no emotion. In all of our meetings, I never saw her smile, laugh, or show the slightest human emotion. The closest she ever came to human emotion appeared when she was deep in thought or when she was asked a personal question. A real piece of work. Her gears turned behind her dead eyes, but she lacked the humanity to function properly with other life forms. Her idea of a personal question? Where are you going for lunch today? Upon her consideration of such a query, she would tax her brain almost to aneurysm, her giant bottom lip creeping up to her nose as if to attempt suicide by face consumption.

"I have some real problems with some of your stories," she finally said, releasing her gigundous bottom lip dropped like a 400-pound man's gut after he releases his belt. Her nose, free at last, from inevitable capture.

"What kind of problems do you have?" I asked sharply.

Her bottom lip started up again then retreated after she noticed me noticing her crazy lip tick.

"You're talking about bar whores and yet your approach is too sterile. I mean, these people are real people, I assume."

"Some of them, yes."

"And these incidents are real, I presume?"

"Yes. Most are taken from my experiences or tales that others have told me."

"Your characters seem too plastic. Your dialogue is rather wooden."

"And?" I cut her off.

A brief silence followed then she began again. "I feel we have something here. I want you to take a few weeks, do some rewrites before I shop it to our publisher."

I sat quietly biting my tongue. I strongly resented her using the word "we" when she talked about "my" book. I prided myself on my interesting characters. The critics praised my use of characters and catchy dialogue to move the story in all their reviews of Visiting Brooklyn. Now this rotund Jew lady was telling me that "our book" had "plastic people with wooden dialogue."

Nancy's bottom lip raced up to her nose again like a snot-nosed two-year-old retreating under his mom's shirt for another shot of milk.

My father, a real character in "Blue Moon," the first short story in my collection, often told me when I was a kid to never do business with Jews. The old man's advice was coming back to haunt me now as I sat across from Nancy Schwartz.

I could walk out and try to get another agent. But who? One book under your belt, you're still considered a rookie and a risk in the publishing business.

Stick it out, do the rewrite and eat the shit that Nancy wants to spoon feed you- I though.

Nancy broke the silence.

"Where are you writing? St. Louis or where?"

I cleared my throat to make sure I didn't give away my raging inferno burning up my insides.

"No, I bought the old family farm in Green County and spent some time writing there."

"Are you crazy?"

"Yeah, I used the money from the book and bought the family farm. I bought the old family farm in Greene County. That's the one," I replied with pride in my voice.

Nancy stared at me, dumbfounded.

"Does your wife know?"

"Well, kinda. I told her I invested all of the money from Visiting Brooklyn, and I did...in land...in the Catskill Mountains." I stared back at her, daring her to say something condescending.

"You're crazier than I ever imagined." She shook her bobble-head.

"Nancy, thanks for the compliment! We Irish people take our craziness very seriously." I remained the bigger person through clenched teeth and my best faux smile.

"I am going to recommend something to you that, speaking of which is going to sound crazy, but at the same time is very sane, given the nature of our new book."

Nancy paused for a moment and pursed her lips together and sucked them in her cavernous mouth. I'd never seen her contort her mouth like that before. I wondered what had brought on this new level of freakiness.

Finally she spoke. "My parents and I used to go to this little resort in Florida. It's outside of Fort Lauderdale. It's not your typical family resort."

She pursed her lips again. "It was a nudist resort." She landed the plane with a big exhale.

"You want me to go to a family nudie park?" My voice cracked. What kind of nut-job am I dealin' with here? The very image of Nancy nude made me want to hurl. But laughing at her was not an option. As a matter of fact, it would get me inked onto the front page of her shit list.

"Look, I feel you need to be relaxed when you write about the people you describe in your stories. The stories are great. You need to feel comfortable with the human body. You write like a Catholic school boy."

"I am a Catholic school boy!" My voice rose. Immediately, I wanted to offer an apology. I started to talk and Nancy shook her head and waved me off.

"I didn't mean to offend you. By the way, I am half Catholic, if that means anything. My mother was Italian and my father was a Jew. Great people! They thought I should pick my own religion. I chose none of the above."

I looked at the wall behind Nancy's desk. A single picture of a very young couple from the 1950s—the woman looked like Connie Francis and the man resembled a young Eddie Fischer. How could a nice-looking couple have a daughter that looked like Nancy?

"Kenny, I mean it. Get away for a week. Try doing some of the rewrites I suggested. I'm telling you, as your agent, go some place other than the Catskill Mountains and your run-down farm. I want you to check this place out, at least for a couple of days."

The meeting ended with Nancy writing down the name and an eight hundred number on a piece of her stationary.

"Kenny, I am serious about you going to this place. It's called Paradise Lake."

She paused to suty me for a brief moment.

"Take a few days to think about it. When you make reservations make sure you tell them you're friends of Harvey and Maria Schwartz. My parents are still legends down there. You'll be treated like gold."

Finally, she stood up and offered her hammy hand. I felt a slight tremor in her right hand. She clasped her left hand over mine and shook with both hands. "Please make it to Paradise Lake," she said with a creepy whisper.

I left her office and somehow I convinced myself I needed to clear my head. Nancy had seemed different this time.

She'd appeared listless and her usual combativeness, absent. Her insistance on me going to the nudie colony was suspect. Most of all, the mention of her parents. The photos behind her desk she never spoke of. Nancy never discussed her family or anything personal. Now she was telling me her parents were nudists, not just run-of-the-mill nudists but renown nudists.

The second thing I pondered was how I was going to tell my wife I'd taken most of the book money and invested it in a never-discussed property acquisition. She's gonna shit! Worst of all, my siblings hated the family farm. No one felt attached to the old place but me.

Occasionally, I'd daydream about some of the changes I hoped to make on the property. Build a new cottage or dig a fish pond. I visited the Greene County farm and saw that those changes were real. I mentioned this to several people and they always steered the conversation away to the weather or last night's TV.

I found one person who understood my affinity for the old family farm. She was the wife of a distant relative in Ireland.

I had finally gotten around to tracking down relatives in Ireland. They lived in a small town in County Roscommon called Elphin. We went to the family farm owned by my distant cousin Conor. My brother, his son, my son, and my grandson made the first trip over to meet our newfound family a few years ago. I got out of the car and scanned around, overwhelmed by a sense of familiarity with the stone stucco house and the emerald green fields. I asked my brother if he felt anything. He said no.

My cousin, Conor, has five kids. My parents had five kids. The family farm in Elphin had been in our family for over 150 years. The same family lived, generation after generation, on the same land, in the same house. We met the family and talked. Even though it was only ten in the morning, Conor offered us all a glass of whiskey, Paddy's whiskey.

After a few sips, Conor offered to give us a tour of the farm. His accent was thick, probably made thicker by his morning whiskey. I explained as best as I could the feeling of familiarity with the surroundings and the feeling of knowing the land and how I sensed I'd been here before, in dreams, at least.

Conor's wife, Mary, overheard the conversation. "Tis is an Irish thing, you know," she offered, matter of fact.

"What is?" I asked.

"Your whole connection with the land. The Irish have always been land starved for generations. Our love of the land comes from the need of land."

We visited the barn and the family horses.

"We had a horse on our farm in upstate New York," I said.

"So you did live on a farm then?" Mary queried.

"Yeah, we had about seventy acres in the middle of the Catskill Mountains. Beautiful place, open fields and a giant green barn."

"It was a grand green barn was it now?" asked Mary.

"It was a giant green barn," I replied.

"You seem to be attached to the land there in New York. Your family still owns the property?" queried Mary.

"No, we gave it up after our parents divorced. It's been divided up several times and now there are summer houses and out-buildings scattered around. Mary, I talk about this to people and get strange stares. But I dream about the old farm. I dream of changes taking place, and when I visit the place, I find out the changes are real."

"And you think you're crazy for this, now?" she asked with a smile.

"Not exactly crazy, but a little odd," I replied meekly.

"Not crazy, not odd, just being a lot Irish, I would think," she said.

Mary grabbed my arm and let the group get a head of us.

"I don't like talkin' this way in front of the kids and Conor. They think I am a loon anyway. But I think what you have is a bit of your ancestry and pagan blood. It was that early Irish before St. Paddy and they all worshipped the land. I think we carry it all with us and now it only peeks out once in a while. The priest and the church don't like to talk about such stuff, but you and I know tis real."

Conor dug up a piece of sod from the field for us to take home, only to get confiscated by customs in New York.

I walked down Second Avenue until I reached Forty-Eighth Street. My father's family had lived between Third and Lexington for over fifty years. The brownstone was torn down in the mid-fifties to make way for a parking garage. My grandmother, aunt, and uncle moved across the street to the Middleton Hotel. They stayed there until they all died in the early seventies. The parking lot was replaced by an imitation brownstone building in the mid-nineties.

Just a walk, I told myself, but I knew exactly where it was leading me.

I cut through the lobby of the Waldorf Astoria, a habit I'd picked up in my youth. When I visited my grandmother's apartment, we would always cut through the Waldorf.

Now on Fiftieth Street I continued west. I needed the exercise, and I needed to decipher what Nancy had said.

"Good God, visiting a nudist camp," I said to myself out loud.

That image of a nude Nancy came to mind again, and I began to crack up. I would have to call my wife and tell her Nancy had suggested I visit Florida for about a week and do some revisions.

I was parallel to St. Patrick's and on the Sak's side of Fiftieth. Mayor Giuliani, in his effort to control New York, had blocked pedestrian traffic crossing Fifth Avenue directly in front of St. Patrick's.

I walked two blocks up Fifth Avenue and stood in front of Borders Books. Six months earlier, I had been in the store with several other new authors for a book signing event a year earlier.

Talk turned to agents then. The young Hispanic graduate student whose book was about going underground as a migrant worker told us her agent was a "godsend."

The young Bronx Jew who'd written about his year working with Palestinian refugees in Gaza,asked what agent I used.

"Nancy Schwartz," I said proudly.

"The East Side Golem herself," he shrieked.

The young Hispanic woman asked what a golem was.

"Well, think of it as a Jewish Frankenstein monster. According to the Kabal, a rabbi can make a monster and set it upon the enemies of his people. The best-known golem in history is the Golem of Prague. Seems the old rabbi got sick of the pogroms so he made himself a golem and it kicked ass all over Prague. In fact, there is a statute of the golem in the old Jewish quarters in Prague."

"You're kidding?" responded the young woman.

"No, he's right. I've seen the statue. The story is a favorite Jewish legend," I said.

"But Nancy Schwartz is real!" the Jew managed to squeeze in.

So my agent was known as the East Side Golem, amongst a gaggle of other names I'm sure. She took me on, a middle-aged first timer, and six months later I was on the best-seller lists and had made some pocket change.

The next time I stopped in Borders, Visiting Brooklyn was on the clearance table reduced by 40 percent.

I picked up a copy for the hell of it and a floor clerk stopped, looked at the back cover, then looked at me.

"Hey, that's you, ain't it?" he asked.

"Yeah, it's me. Just checking out the merchandise and seeing how sales are going."

"Just got a few left. Why don't ya hang around and see if you can push it to some customers?"

This visit, my book was not on the clearance table. I went to the information desk and asked if they had Visiting Brooklyn. The young female clerk never looked up but simply said, "Tourism books are on the second floor."

"Excuse me, miss, but Visiting Brooklyn is a novel, and I just want to know if you have any copies on the floor."

She put down her magazine and demanded, "Author's name and title, please."

I gave her both.

"We have three copies in the store. Go to the fiction suspense area behind these stairs and you'll find it."

I thanked her with mock sarcasm in my voice and walked toward the front door.

Nancy was right. You're forgotten quickly in the book business. You need to crank them out and keep your name in the spotlight or you'll die a quick death.

With that ritual over, I had to make a choice. Go upstate and visit my brother and the farm or go home to St. Louis. I knew if I went home, I wouldn't make it to Nancy's family favorite nudie resort. I could skip upstate, tell my wife that I wanted to spend some time with my brother.

I went out on Fifth Avenue and hailed a cab.

"LaGuardia, Delta, please," I said to the cabbie.

I had no idea what time the Delta shuttle left for Albany. I could spend my time reviewing Nancy's notes and make the necessary corrections. My computer bag acted as my overnight bag with shaving and basic meds. A few days in Albany, a new set of clothes, not a big deal.

On the way out to the airport, I called my wife, told her I'd met with Nancy and she had some revisions I needed to work on. I told her I'd spend a few days upstate with my brother and try to get the rewrites finished, then I'd visit the farm the next day.

The cabby was some flavor of middle-eastern. After 9/11 it was no longer politically correct to ask cabbies where they were from.

He couldn't carry a conversation in English, but he sure had his hustle down pat. "Twenty-five dollars plus tip!" Of course. There was his English.

I handed him a twenty and a ten and told him to keep the change. I had barely pulled my hand away from the window when he sped off. You're entirely welcome, you son of a bitch.

The skycaps recoiled after the cab departed and there I stood with only my computer case. As I pulled the case up on my shoulder, I felt the heft several pounds of paper made.

At the Delta counter, I asked, "When is the next flight to Albany?"

"We have a flight at four thirty, but it's full. The next flight departs at six."

It was one o'clock. Three and half hour of writing and drinking Guinness in the bar. I could handle that. Five hours was a little much.

I could rent a car and drive up to Albany.

On impulse, I asked. "When is your next flight to Fort Lauderdale?"

"We have a shuttle that leaves on the hour. You can catch the next flight out at two o'clock. Would you like that?"

I nodded with a smile and pushed my driver's license and MasterCard toward the ticket agent.

The agent took her time examining my driver's license. She looked at me then my driver's license picture twice.

Lone man wants to go to Albany then changes his mind and asks about Fort Lauderdale. No luggage to check.

"Look, I know it looks bad, me wanting to change destinations that quickly, but I have to go to Florida anyway. You see I am a writer and—"

"Hey mister, you're okay, you are okay."

I knew I was babbling, so I gave her a simple thank you and she handed me a ticket.

"Gate D-6. Have a nice trip." She smiled politely and motioned for the next person in line.

In Fort Lauderdale, the middle-aged blonde at the Avis counter casually asked me where I was headed. "I'm going to a resort a few miles out of town. A place called Lake Paradise. Ever heard of it?"

Her face lit up with an expression that bordered on a blush and a sneer.

"Yeah, I've heard of it. I believe it's what they call a naturalist resort. Follow the signs for I-95 until you see signs for the Florida Turnpike, aka Alligator Alley. Take it west for about thirty miles and..." Her voice drifted off as she outlined my route with yellow marker on the map.

"So you're familiar with Lake Paradise?" I asked as I took the map.

"Only by reputation."

"And?"

A genuine smile came to her face.

"Look, a few years back the place had a reputation as kind of wild, if you know what I mean. A scandal over drugs or something. Now it's supposedly mellowed out. Lots of old people." Her face soured at the thought. "But the locals still talk about the old days. When Lake Paradise is mentioned around here, people will either pray for your soul or wish they were going with you." The blonde gave me a nod, a wink, and a smile that indicated our conversation was finished.

For all of our trips to Florida, our family had never left the beach resorts. Now I headed into the Everglades with mixed feelings of impending doom and titilating adventure.

The road turned from the smooth blacktop to dusty gray gravel in no time. I slowed the light blue Charger down to minimize the dust. At the entrance the sign read "Welcome To Lake Paradise - A Family Nudist Resort - You May Encounter Naked People Here Because This Is a Clothing Optional Area." Good Lord, what am I doing here?

My car creeped up to the guard shack, a white pole blocking the entrance. An old lady stepped out onto the gravel. Her naked body, deeply tanned and full of deep wrinkles, instantly offended my senses. Her hair was snow white and arranged in a large bun on the top of her head.

"Welcome to Lake. Are you visiting one of our residents or are you a guest?" She waited for a reply.

I must have stared at her longer than I should have. She said, "Sonny, you take your time. I don't get many people staring at me much anymore. I kinda like it, if you know what I mean!"

Oh my God! I tried to shake her raisined image out of my head. "I'm sorry I must have—" I stammered.

"Son, don't be sorry just be glad there's places like this where people don't give a good goddamn what you look like, just as long as everyone else is naked."

She managed to put about three k's in the word naked.

"I am here as a guest. I need to check in," I spoke into my steering wheel as I kept my eyes on my shoes.

"Pull up and park in the visitor parking lot. Go to the reception area, they'll get you checked in. And one other thing, sonny. Get yourself a good set of sunglasses. It makes your staring less obvious and a lot more fun." The crinkled woman stepped back and waved me through.

I pulled the rental car into a parking space and headed for the reception area. The lady behind the counter was topless, past sixty, and her bright red hair, thin and disheveled, revealed a very sun-burnt scalp. She'd arranged her curls to hide bald spots. Her breasts hung like empty feed sacks staring at her toes. Learning from my guard shack incident, I stared directly at a bald spot in the middle of her forehead.

"Can I help you?" she offered without the hospitality that had greeted me at the guard gate.

"I need a room for about a week," I said as I scanned the lobby. I tried to mentally erase the cock-blocking visions in my head.

"You got reservations, right?" she barked.

"Reservations?" My voice cracked as I repeated the word and honed in on her eyes.

"Yeah, I believe it's a French word. You usually call ahead to see if rooms are available."

My eyes tracked from her eyes to her bald spot at her temple to her pruned lips. The red lipstick looked like a three-year-old had applied it and was offset by clown-like pink rouge circles on her cheeks. Frightening, really.

"My friend...excuse me...I mean, my literary agent, Nancy Schwartz, told me to mention her name and to say I was a friend of hers and Harvey and Maria Schwartz." I blinked my eyes for a long few seconds. Hopefully this whole place was just a dream. Nope.

The red-headed dried apricot with a painted face paused, looking upset. Tears swelled in her eyes and cut a wet path through her labyrinth of wrinkles under her eyes.

She cleared her throat and dabbed her face with a tissue. Her heavy Jersey accent came out "For God's sake, why couldn't ya tell me you were friends of Harv and Maria?"

."I'm sorry. Did I say something...I just wanted a room." I was mortified.

"I'm sorry, but the Schwartzes are saints here." As she spoke, she made the sign of the cross and kissed her thumb.

I tried again. "Nancy just told me to mention her family."

"Tell me, how is our girl, little Nancy?"

I almost laughed but pinched my lips between my teeth. Given the lady's fragile emotions, I held back my smart-ass comments.

"Nancy is fine. As I said, she's my literary agent."

She finally checked me in. I took the opportunity to look around the reception area. A small gift shelf on one wall had t-shirts and postcards advertising Lake Paradise, typical tourist junk.

The redhead made copies of my driver's license and credit card and returned to the counter.

"Would you have any shorts?" I asked meekly.

"No market for shorts here, mister. We usually suggest the dress towel for 'newbies.' It's a fancy towel with snaps. You can wear it like a bottom toga. Right behind you, bottom shelf." Old sea salt pointed them out.

I reached for the bottom shelf and retrieved what appeared to be a small towel with a sunset.

"Check the size, mister. Nothing like trying to get into a towel that's too small."

"It says extra large," I pointed out.

"You're not that big. It should be okay. And you're in luck. They're on sale for fifteen dollars, usually twenty-two. I can charge it to your room if you'd like." I signed the registration sheet and the credit card receipt.

Old sea salt reached for a walkie-talkie and announced, "Mandy, we got us a newbie and a white tail up at reception." She released the button and waited for a response.

"Gotcha. I'll be right outside."

The screen door to the reception room opened and another naked lady walked in.

Unlike the first two, this one appeared to be in her late forties or early fifties. Her body was solid like an aged athlete who hadn't let herself go. It took me a moment to realize that the naked lady had only one breast. Her right as flat folded skin. Her left breast appeared to be a healthy C-cup.

The woman approached me with her hand out. "Good evening. I am Mandy. My friends call me Unicorn or Uni for short."

"Nice to meet you, Mandy. My name is Ken."

Mandy called over my shoulder to the redhead. "Margie, where is Kenny Boy staying?"

"The House," Old sea salt replied.

Mandy looked into my face. "So, we appear to have a big shot here today!"

I opened my mouth to speak, but Mandy beat me to it.

"No, you don't understand. Anyone who stays in the house has to be connected to the Schwartzes somehow. Never met them, but they are like saints around here so enjoy the celebrity status while you can."

I smiled and accepted my fate.

"Got any luggage in your car?" she inquired.

"Nope, this is it," I said holding up my computer bag and wrap-around towel.

Again she called over my shoulder to old saggy bags. "I thought you told me this newbie was a white tail?"

"He is, trust me."

We settled into the gold golf cart headed toward a group of bungalows surrounded by travel trailers and permanently affixed mobile homes.

"I can figure out what a newbie is, but what the hell is a 'white tail?'"

"Ever see yourself or your significant other after you been out in the sun with a bathing suit on?" she asked.

"Yeah."

"Well, your ass is white and the rest of you is tanned, thus the phrase 'white tail.' We use 'newbies' to describe someone new to the resort. We use 'white tail' for those who have never shown their bare arses in public. So when you show up here with only a computer case and a towel, I figured you for a newbie but not a white tail."

"I'm definitely a white tail, for sure!"

She drove the golf cart through the resort. My first impression of the place formed when Mandy said, "Kinda like an Arkansas FEMA trailer village meets army barracks, ain't it?"

She was right. The long white barrack-like buildings gave way to a smattering of campers and mobile homes. Each individual lot had its own take on flowers and shrubbery. Behind each lot were giant pines that shaded the rear of the mobile homes and travel trailers.

"What's with all the pines?"

She replied with the song, "In the pines, in the pines, where the sun never shines in the pines."

"Loretta Lynn?"

"Very good. You must be a fan."

"Not really. I just know that song."

"The pines provide shade for the homes in the late afternoon when the sun is a real bitch. I mean, as much as these folks love the sun, summer down here can be brutal. When they laid this place out they made sure the streets and trees provided proper shade."

Mandy made a sharp left turn and her bare breast brushed across the middle of my right arm. I immediately pulled away and sat up straight as the gold cart righted itself on a straight away. She immediately sensed my embarrassment.

"Look, she don't bite. No, she's the best little girl in the world. Now her sister, she was the nasty one. You see what they done to her!"

It was one of those awkward moments when I didn't know if I should laugh or what. She laughed at herself.

"I didn't mean to make you unconformable or anything. I just need to get used to this place," I said, trying to make up for not laughing with her. "How long does it take to get used to being nude?"

"Kenny Boy, just relax. That's the best part of being naked all the time. You just let it all go."

We pulled up to a small cottage that looked more like a country cottage from the Catskill Mountains—blue siding with light blue shutters and a white picket fence. The small lawn was surrounded by flower beds. The walk-up to the door was made of dark gray slate slabs, .The type of gray slate you'd see in New York not in Florida.

"Welcome to The House. I guess they call it The House because it's the only traditional building at Paradise Lake. It was built by Harvey and Marie Schwartz. It's something of memorial. It's used by special friends of the Schwartz family. Since you're staying in it, folks here will assume you have a close connection to the Schwartzes."

"Their daughter, Nancy, is my literary agent," I said.

"So you're a celebrity in your own right?"

"I only have one novel published. I'm down here to work on my second endeavor."

"What's the name of your novel?"

"*Visiting Brooklyn*."

"Never heard of it, but that doesn't mean much. I'm pretty much a television fan."

"It's kinda a thriller-romance. Russian mafia meets the New York Italian mafia. The main character is an Irishman."

"Sounds too complicated for me already," she said.

"What now?" I asked.

"Well, this is the point that I rip your clothes off and violate you," said Mandy.

The sheepish grin on her face put me at ease.

"Well, first of all, we get you undressed and get on with the tour of the place. That means you sneak into your cottage and shed the textiles, slip into your little terry loin cloth, and grab a towel."

"A towel?" I asked.

"Yes, naked etiquette one oh one: When naked, always have a towel in tow."

"I don't get it."

"Look, Kenny Boy, let me put it as bluntly as possible. Nobody wants to sit down where your bare ass has been. No one wants to see slide marks. You go naked, you bring a towel."

As Mandy smiled, I noticed she was missing a tooth. I immediately felt accepted. If a woman can run naked and care less about a missing breast, why should a missing tooth bother her?

"Look, champ, let's get going or we'll miss happy hour at the Butt Crack."

"Come again. The Butt Crack?"

"Yeah, we got a little bar here and it's called the Butt Crack Bar. Most of the old timers come out for happy hour because the drinks are cheap. Tonight, everyone's favorite bartender is working and that's always a draw, so get naked and let's get a move on."

I went into the master bedroom to change into my towel. I would go naked at some point this week, but I closed the door out of habit.

The room was sparse with a large king bed, a giant bureau, and a writing desk with chair. The floor was stone tile. I knew from previous trips to Florida that rugs and carpets didn't fair well in the tropical climate. Once naked, I looked for a mirror. I wanted to check the whiteness of my ass before I unveiled it to the public. No mirrors. I opened a door to the bathroom. The angle of the medicine cabinet mirror was too high to provide a view of my ass. I opened the other door which led to a girl's room. A twin bed rounded out the soft feminine decor. I felt like I was in someone's daughter's bedroom rather than a guest house.

I walked to the bed, checked out my white ass in the mirror, and noticed a picture, a black and white photo of man and woman with a young girl. A typical family portrait with the exception they were all naked. I looked closer at the photo and realized the man and woman were Nancy's parents, Harvey and Marie. But who was the pretty young girl? I picked up the photo, and walked out the door to the living room.

Mandy seemed confused by me entering through a different door.

"Mandy, just one question. I know these people are Harvey and Marie Schwartz, but who is the pretty young thing in the middle?"

Her carefree spirit disappeared, replaced by suspicion.

"Look, fella, you come here." She started to grab at me.

"No, no, Nancy Schwartz is my agent, and she sent me down here." I tried to defend myself.

"Okay, she's your agent and you ask who the pretty young thing is in the picture? It may be an old picture, but I think you should recognize Nancy Schwartz when you see her."

"Oh, no, I know Nancy Schwartz, and that is not her." I turned to go back to the girl's bedroom.

Mandy came in tow.

I walked to the writing desk and picked up the picture frame. I studied it closely, the faces of the family members. The mother and father were definitely the same people in the photo from Nancy's office.

But the girl? How could this beautiful girl be Nancy Schwartz? Nancy was well over six feet. Though the adults in the picture appeared tall, the girl was average height, just a few inches shorter than the mother. The girl was slender and athletic, like both of her parents. If any child took the best from both parents in gene selection, the girl in the picture did.

Mandy, right behind me, spoke. "Well, what do you think? Is that your Nancy or what?"

I paused for a moment and pictured the Nancy Schwartz I'd seen that morning.

"The lady I know is over six feet tall. She weights over two hundred pounds and is extremely unattractive. I don't know how this pretty gal could be my Nancy Schwartz."

"Tell you what, Kenny Boy. We can go up to the Butt Crack and you can buy me a drink. Some of the old timers can give you the lowdown on the Schwartzes. We can finish our tour tomorrow. How's about it?" she said.

I placed the picture back on the desk.

"You're right, a drink would be great, and talking to some of the old timers may clear things up."

As Mandy headed out the cottage door she called over her shoulder for me not to forget my sitting towel.

Mandy took the long route to the Butt Crack. She explained that Lake Paradise was a nudist commune. The prices for rentals and maintenance were kept down because each member worked a certain number of hours to maintain the property and offset the costs. Since she paid for her lot rental and membership, she did the minimum eight hours a week. She had a day off tomorrow and wanted me to get comfortable before the locals met me.

We did a quick tour of the recreation areas that included tennis courts, bocce courts, and volleyball. She zoomed through the nature area set aside for wildlife and local fauna.

We stopped in front of a small building that resembled an old chicken coup.

"What's this?" I asked.

"Don't let appearances fool you, Kenny Boy. This here is the world famous Butt Crack Bar."

Mandy hopped from her cart and led the way through the screen door. The door was less than six feet. I ducked my head and stepped inside.

The threshold changed from concrete sidewalk to sand under my toes. Before I could get oriented to my new surroundings, Mandy grabbed my arm and guided me to a bar stool.

Only two other people besides us were in the bar; the gal from the front gate sat on the corner stool. Her leathery flesh drooped from her boney body. A lady in her early forties was behind the bar, topless and with a towel wrap.

My towel wrap had a sunset. Hers had some type of American Indian design on the rear and the face of an Indian woman on the front.

Mandy introduced the bartender first.

"Layla, this here's a new guest. Just call him Kenny Boy."

"Well, welcome to our little home here in the swamps," replied Layla.

Her voice was very southern.

I was going to ask her about her roots but Mandy beat me to it. "Old Layla's family is the original Florida crackers with a little Seminole Indian thrown in. Right, sweetie?"

"Yeah, the family goes way far back. Family history has it that one of my injun relatives almost killed old Andy Jackson when he tried to clean the Indians out of Florida."

I noticed when Layla spoke she didn't look at the person she talked to. Rather she kept herself in motion dusting bottles, wiping the counter.

Three old men entered the bar and sat at the far end by the door. I noticed the back wall behind them was draped by American and Canadian flags. It was the only solid wall. The rest of the bar consisted of screen. The bar reminded me of a family's screened-in back porch. A poor family's back porch at that.

The first old man shouted his order at Layla. "Hey, Indian Princess, give me one of them Miller Lites, will ya now?" His voice was deep and very East Coast New York or Jersey.

Layla looked at the other two and they shook their heads no. The bartender leaned deep into the cooler to pull out the Miller Lites. As she bent over, the three old men placed their elbows on the bar, leaned as close as they could to the barmaid's exposed bare ass. As soon a she straightened up, they returned to their positions.

Layla returned to Mandy and me. "Well folks, what'll it be?"

Mandy ordered a Coke with no ice.

"Too early for you?" I asked.

"No, I am one of them strange creatures who doesn't drink. No religion, alcoholism, abusive parents, or crazy uncle. I just never developed a taste for booze. I'm happy with my Cokes."

I ordered a Jameson on the rocks with club soda on the side.

"Say, Kenny Boy, you a real Irishman or what?" asked Mandy.

"One hundred percent! I even have an Irish passport," I added.

Layla had our drinks in front of us, and chatted about her horses and life in the swamps.

One of the old men shouted to her, "Hey, Princess, give me a Miller Lite, will ya dear?" This accent was definitely Bostonian.

Layla went to the end the bar, again bent over the cooler to retrieve a Miller Lite. The old men simultaneously placed their elbows on the bar, just as before, and checked out the barmaid's ass.

I asked Mandy, "Does she realize what those guys are doing?"

She looked at me and smiled. Not a big smile that revealed her missing tooth but rather a courtesy smile. She tried to convey that I really shouldn't concern myself with the situation. "Kenny Boy, let me tell you, when you get old like those guys, it just takes a little peep to bring them a little gratification. Those old guys come in here every afternoon at the same time, ogle the same way with whoever is on duty. Silly? Yes! But it's a safe amusement."

"I guess I don't get it. They see naked people all day, why would they want to look at someone's ass?"

"They look because it's naughty. It's taboo. Layla knows what they're doing. She purposely plunges into the ice chest to give the old guys their thrill for the day. They'll drink three beers, space them out so she has to bend over every time. No harm done."

I wanted to measure my words lest I make another assumption about people and a lifestyle I didn't understand. "I just thought the nudist community had some standards. You know, something like 'nude, not rude.'"

Mandy shot back, "Our motto here is, 'Nude, not prude.' You'll find the folks here at Lake Paradise like their sex like anybody, that is, if they can still get it up. Viagra has been a godsend for some of these old goats!" She ended with a cackle.

"Speaking of prude...what happens when one of us 'white tails' get a little excited and..."

She cut me off. "Oh, you mean if you get a woody in front of people? Well, the first time you get a warning. The second offense, you get it whacked off and we display it in that pickle jar over the bar." She pointed to a giant jar between the liquor bottles. Mandy noticed I was studying the jar to see if those pickles were really pickles.

"That was a joke!"

I gripped my towel skirt with two hands and sighed a deep breath of relief.

"I'm just fuckin' with you, man!" She shook her head.

"I know, I just felt it was my time to mess with you, that's all," I said as I looked off behind the bar awkwardly.

We both laughed and she hugged me, her bare breast in the middle of my naked back. "Watch that or I may become a candidate for the pickle jar."

She pulled up my towel and examined my crotch. "Nope. Not yet. Still got a ways to go."

"Hey!" I shouted as I yanked my towel back over my package.

"You know I'll keep my eye on it over the next few days," she laughed.

The third old man ordered his Miller Lite and Mandy knew it was time to start the conversation.

"Gentlemen," she addressed the old men. "We have an honored and distinguished guest among us. Kenny Boy, here, is staying in The House and he's a dear friend of Nancy Schwartz."

One by one the old men strolled over and introduced themselves.

The first seat belonged to Mike, a retired New York City firefighter.

Second seat was Pete, a retired teacher from Boston.

The third belonged to Mo, a New Jersey boy who owned an accounting firm.

The three began a barrage of questions about Nancy.

Mandy held up her hands, demanding silence.

"Look, boys, Kenny has some questions too. So why don't we let him start, okay? You know, like one at a fuckin' time. Just one of you ask your question and Kenny will answer, then he'll ask you a question and so on and so on." All three of the old men nodded in submission to Mandy.

She went on like a school teacher. "Since Kenny Boy is an honored guest, we should let him ask the first question. Fair?"

Again they nodded.

"Mike. Pete. Mo. Nice to meet you all. Like Mandy said, I'm here for a couple days to finish some revisions on my second novel. Nancy is my literary agent. My first question...there's a picture of the Schwartzess in my room and the young lady—"

Mo interrupted right away. "That young lady is Nancy Schwartz."

"But the Nancy Schwartz I know is over six feet tall and, well, the kindest thing I can say is that she's extremely unattractive. The girl in the photograph is petite and pretty."

Pete spoke up. "Yeah, it seems that Nancy had some disease that caused her to grow and become deformed. We're no medical experts, but we call it 'gigantism.'"

Mike chimed in. "Our turn, Kenny Boy. How is our little Nancy?"

"As I said, she's my literary agent. I guess she's fine. I saw her this morning and she looked...like she normally does."

"How can you say she's fine when you said earlier that she's ugly?" shouted Mo.

"Hey Jew boy, take it easy on our new guest," Mike responded.

"Look, you drunken mick, we got someone here who just visited our little Nancy and you want me to be nice. I want answers, and I don't want anyone tellin' me she's ugly."

"Extremely unattractive. There's a difference." Pete defended.

"What the fuck's the difference?" asked Mo.

Mandy raised both hands and called for order. "Boys, come on, give us a break here. Let Kenny Boy tell you what he knows without rude interruptions."

The old guys settled down, and I began. "Well, there's not much to tell. Nancy has been my agent for the last two years. She pushed my first book, Visiting Brooklyn, to the best-seller list and now I'm working on my second book. We never met socially or anything. But I can tell you she's a hell of an agent." Spoken like a true politician.

"So she's too ugly for you? Were you ashamed to be with her in public?" Mo ranted.

"No, not at all. Nancy is all business. The closest we ever came to getting personal was her telling me to come down here. She wanted me to meet real people, I guess. People who knew her and her family," I replied, still unsure why I was here.

Mike spoke up. "Hey look, fella, our little Nancy hasn't been here for close to twenty-five years. She stopped comin' when she started to change. Now she starts sending her friends down. Somethin' must be up."

The three old men gulped their Miller Lites.

"I don't mean to be rude, but what the hell are you old fuckers talkin' about?" Mandy asked.

Pete responded. "Unicorn, there are some things that are part of this club's history. Your friend here, Kenny Boy, has just brought us something from the past that we need to talk about,"

"Okay, for God's sake, who's gonna bring us latter-day newbies up-to-date history on your past?" Mandy questioned.

Pete started to speak, but Mo cut him off.

"Look, Harvey was a member of my tribe and I should get to tell the story."

Pete shot back, "And his wife, Maria, she was one of my people, Italian. So I can't talk?"

"Tell you what, I tell the first part of the story and you finish, capiche?" Mo said, with genuine kindness in his voice.

"And you promise to not cut me off, old codger?" said Pete playfully.

"Oh, I promise on your mother's eye," replied Mo.

Mo began the story of Harvey and Marie Schwartz and Lake Paradise.

"Harv and Marie were both professors of literature at NYU. Harvey's family had money connected to the publishing industry. Over the years, Harvey managed to acquire several small publishing houses that would be purchased by the big boys.

"His wealth grew, as well as his influence in the bookworm world. Both Marie and Harvey had one passion outside their books and teaching, naturalism. In the fifties, places like Lake Paradise were known as nudist colonies rather than resorts. There were a few places in the Catskills, but in the winter months there were no places to go up north. If you're at all familiar with the Catskills, you'll notice the resemblance between The House and some of the older places in the Catskills."

Mo continued with his story.

"So, Harvey and Marie decided they needed someplace else for themselves and their nudist friends during the winter. Lake Paradise was a virtual swamp when Harv and Marie bought the land in the late fifties. They both took sabbaticals for a year and came down here to set the place up, with help from fellow nudists from the Northeast, including yours truly and my fellas here. We spent our vacations helping Harv and Marie build this place. The first years, we only had tents and a few trailers. The bungalows were built first and then The House.

"It was supposed to be a model for other buildings at Lake Paradise, but God intervened, so to speak. The local Baptist Church got wind of some Yankees coming here to spread sin among the locals. They got the county government to stop issuing building permits. Thus the time warp of early Catskills schlock in the building design. The only way we survived was through a loophole in the law allowing temporary camping, what the ordinances described as 'travel trailers.' A place once created to be an exclusive nudist resort was now reduced to a fucking trailer park. But we outsmarted the Bible thumpers. As the mobile home industry increased along with RV's, we were able to get bigger and better rigs in here. Some of the oldies remain. We managed to survive."

Mo wiped his brow and took another slug of his beer.

"What about Harvey and Marie?" I asked.

"Too emotional for me. I'll let the Mick and the Guinea take over," replied Mo.

"Gee thanks for the great introduction, you fucking Christ-killing bastard!" Mike yelled back.

"So, what are friends for?" Mo said.

"Just like a fuckin' Jew to answer a question with a question," said Pete.

Mike signaled to Layla for another round for him and his friends. They spared the barmaid another gawking routine. Mike went directly into the story.

With a fresh beer in his hands. He cleared his throat several times and took a long swallow of his Miller Lite.

"Maria hated to fly. They only flew down a couple of times—she'd practically have to drug herself into a coma. Finally Harv gave in and drove. He generally tried to drive straight through, no stops. Another thing about Maria, she always wanted to make several stops along the way and break up the drive. Harv wanted none of that. They were the most loving couple in the world, except when it came to travel. Harv always drove the big cars. He liked Oldsmobiles and Buicks. He'd go on about how safe the big cars were, especially when driving down I-95.

"It was early summer of 1983, they were on their way down. As usual, Harv insisted on driving straight through from the city. It was early morning, about six a.m., just outside of West Palm, when the accident happened. We never heard if Harv had fallen asleep or someone ran them off the road, but they both died. They were about fifty miles from the place they loved."

Mike swollowed hard and continued.

I looked at the group of old men. Their moods had gone from playful and raunchy to sullen and withdrawn as Mike told his story.

They were reliving Harv and Maria's deaths as if it were just the day before rather than twenty-five years ago.

Mike tried to speak but managed only to clear his throat and take another sip of his beer. He turned his head and wiped a single tear from his right eye.

"Gentleman," I began, "if this is too much, I can always…"

Mo interrupted me. "Look, it's never a fuckin' good time to talk about the accident. If this weepy Mick can't finish the story, maybe Pete and I need to take over."

"Listen, you mockie, Christ-killin', Jew-bag, son of a bitch, if you think you can tell the story better you go right ahead. Just like your kind took over New York, Israel, and the damn financial markets and Wall Street…" He trailed off with his insults.

Mike was going to continue, but Mo cut him off with, "Mikey, I just wanted to make sure we are still friends, you Goddamn fucking alcoholic Irish bastard." A broad grin broke over Mo's red face after he stopped yelling at his friend.

Pete cut in. "Hey, loverboys, save it for the bedroom. We have a guest of Harv, Marie, and Little Nancy here and he wants to hear the story. So are you guys gonna kiss and make up, or what?" asked Pete.

"Hey, you know us, Pete, a little spat and we're friends, especially when Mo takes out his teeth," replied Mike.

Mo thought of more to say, but Pete raised his hands and the bar got quiet.

Pete took over. "Anyway, after the accident, we found out more about Little Nancy. Remember this was the most beautiful little girl in the world."

Mo interrupted. "And very smart, too."

"Yeah, she was brilliant, too," replied Pete as he continued the story. "We noticed that there were some little changes in Nancy after puberty started to kick in. Things that stood out. Her nose seemed to grow overnight—her feet and hands seemed to be too large for her body. By the time she was sixteen, she came down with her parents but would seldom take her clothes off or leave her parents' cottage. Then she stopped coming. Everyone asked about her, and Harv and Marie would simply say that she was at camp or summer school at her private girl's college in Vermont. She showed up for our memorial service we had for her parents. By this time, Little Nancy was about twenty or twenty-one. We hadn't seen her for almost five years."

After another swig he continued. "Like I said, we hadn't seen her for over five years. None of us were ready for what we saw. This little pretty girl we called Little Nancy was not so little anymore. She had grown to over six feet tall. Her hands and feet were enormous. But the worst part, her face. Once a little princess, she now looked like a gargoyle from a scary movie. Her eyes seemed to have shifted deep into her head. Her lips were chunky and red. When she talked, you couldn't help but notice that her once prefect teeth were now crooked and with grossly receded gums.

"At first, no one recognized her. We thought maybe she was a relative of Harv's and Marie's. But when she approached one of the managers and said she needed to retrieve things from her parents' cottage, well, you can imagine what people were saying. She only stayed around for a few hours. When she left, David Kampawitz called a general meeting. David was head of internal medicine at Miami Zion. He opened with a few words on Harv and Marie and immediately went to Little Nancy's condition.

"He said it was a rare disease that caused the pituitary gland to go into overdrive. Some people call it 'gigantism' but according to the doc that wasn't the proper term. He said she had the early stages of something called Acromegaly. Nancy's case was diagnosed very early in her life. Like when she was about twelve or so. That's rare because the onset is usually occurs in middle-aged adults.

"So here are her parents with a choice to make. Try to get some help for their little girl now or wait until she is older and the disease is in full throttle.

"According to David, Harv and Marie went to some research clinic where they tried experimental drugs that would stop the disease from progressing. The clinic experienced something like eighty percent success. Obviously, Nancy was not a success.

"Instead of slowing the Acromegaly, it sped it up. The Schwartzes were dealing with symptoms of a disease affecting their teenage daughter that should not have happened until she was in her thirties or forties.

"Harv and Marie confided in David and asked him to keep their problem confidential."

The group remained silent.

Mo raised his hand to Layla and made a sign to get three more drinks for him and his bar buddies.

As Layla retrieved the drinks from the cooler box, the old guys once again leaned over the bar to gape at her.

My only thought was that life does go on and a cute butt should never be passed up.

I raised my hand to Layla after she took care of the old men.

I wanted to structure my questions so the old men wouldn't be offended, while at the same time get some insight into the lady who had taken me on as a writer.

"Gentlemen, one more question, if you don't mind?"

"It'll cost you a quarter," Mo said, humoring himself.

Mike got right back in to the fray with Mo. "Fucking kike, you always have to bring money into everything."

Pete raised his hands again. Calm was restored.

"I guess the question is this, why did Nancy want me to come down here? I mean, to her, it was important that I find out about this place."

Mo spoke first. "Son, we're old men. Old people try to tell young people how wise they are. You know us old fuckers really know everything, just ask us. But seriously, you coming here does bring up good and bad emotions in us. The good is good. The bad is this—Nancy sent you down here because she trusts you."

The old men nodded their heads in agreement.

Mo considered his words before he spoke. He stared at the label of his Miller Lite before he took a drink. "Ken Boy, the second part of the riddle is this, our little Nancy sent you down here because she's dying."

With Mo's words, Pete scanned the bar and gazed out the rusty screen door.

Mike pinched the bridge of his noise to avoid the onset of tears.

I couldn't believe what I'd just heard. "What?" I shook my head in disbelief. "What the hell do you mean, dying? I just left Nancy in New York this morning. She seemed fine. I mean, this is the lady who made me…" I stopped talking because I realized panic was creeping into my voice.

Their dear Nancy, an object of love and affection. To me, she was an agent who'd made me a relative success. Her dying meant the end of my writing career. How could I be so selfish?

I regained my composure, took a sip of my drink, cleared my throat.

"I'm sorry, guys, I'm just as upset as you are, but why do you think she's dying? And, why did she send me?"

Mike said, "Look, kid. I'm sure Nancy meant a lot to you but in a different way. She made you a successful author, but you'd had to have some talent or she wouldn't have wasted her time on you. Her dying is going to mean you gotta change agents. To us, it means the end of a family who made all this possible."

"Yeah, kid, you're the fucking messenger," said Pete.

"Back off, guys," replied Mo. "Nancy trusted this man enough to have him come and met her family. So she probably has some other plans for him too. We can speculate all we want about the purpose of your mission, but Nancy wanted you down here. First, to do some rewrites and, second, to meet her family. If she's going to die, she sent her messenger. So let's live with it."

Mo got up from the bar first and said his goodnights to his friends, myself, and Uni.

Pete followed. He waved his hand and said, "Mo's right, guys. Our friend here was sent with a purpose, so let's make sure he does his rewrites and treat him like family." Mike walked out with Pete.

Uni and I were left alone at the bar with Layla.

She tried to make small talk about her horses when Uni raised her hand and announced that she was heading back to her golf cart to make a final round before turning in.

"Ken Boy, think you can make it back The House to on your own?"

"Yeah, let me sit here for a few minutes and clear my head," I said.

Layla started to speak again, but I looked up at her, emotionally drained. I smiled, got up to leave, told her good night.

"Mr. Ken, please don't leave. You're the last one here and ain't nobody gonna show up. I'll be here for another hour or so and I just can't stand—"

I cut her off with, "Okay, okay. I'll behave if you'll behave."

"Who said anything about behaving anyways?" said Layla, her smile sincere.

"As you may have caught on from the ring on my finger, I am married, so behaving is something that I usually do." My voice cracked. I was embarrassed about sounding weak or what wse use to call pussy whipped.

"Look, Mr. Ken, the only thing I really want is company. You deal with them old fuckers long enough and you get suicidal. I mean, how much can you hear about dead people and dicks that don't work before you wonder, 'What the fuck am I doing here?'"

"So why do you work here?"

"I hate being alone. I mean, I really need to be around people, just to listen, do a little talkin'. Please don't tell anyone, but when I don't have overnight guests at home, I sometimes sleep in the barn with my horse because I can't stand to be alone. I really don't like people that much. I just need to know someone's around. Am I crazy, or what?"

"I don't think you're crazy, just a lonely lady who's trying to find her way."

"Seems you found yourself writing those books."

"Writing is something that came to me later in life. I just enjoy it."

"The book you're writing now?"

"It's called Bar Whores. It's a collection of short stories. Some are biographical and some are fictional."

"Will you ever tell which are which?"

"Never!"

Layla reached for a bottle of Jameson's and placed it on the bar with two glasses.

"I usually don't drink with customers, but for you I'll make an exception."

"Why's that?" I asked.

"Cause I want you to put me in your book, silly." She raised her glass and rolled her eyes triumphantly. She then came from behind the bar onto the sand floor. She placed her hand on her side and undid her skirt. She held the skirt above her head and made several turns. He body was nice, less a few stretch marks that appeared to be a few shades lighter than her tanned body.

"Not bad for an older girl, hey, cowboy?"

"You're a very attractive woman."

"Attractive enough to be in your book?"

"The book's not done yet."

Layla placed her skirt over the barstool and climbed on.

"So, cowboy, since I am not wearin' any clothes, you gotta be the bartender in case anyone should walk in. Speaking of bartending, why ain't you poured me a drink yet?"

I grabbed the Jameson's and poured. My hand shook.

"Hey, cowboy, somethin' got you shook up, don't it?" said Layla as she placed her left hand over mine, steadying my hand as I poured the whiskey.

"Guess I'm not use to sitting in a bar alone with a naked lady." I said with a reedy voice.

"Hell, happens all the time around here, cowboy."

"One question?"

"Your quarter, cowboy," Laya replied playfully.

"Why are you callin' me cowboy?"

"Cause I plan on riding you home!"

The next morning Mandy woke me up with a small carafe of coffee next to my bed and a note.

Time to get up, sleepy head. Your guest left
about five this morning. Had to feed her horses.
See you at the snack bar for breakfast.
Uni

My first reaction was absolute panic at the thought of cheating on my wife. How did Mandy know that Layla spent the night? But more important, what the hell went on last night?

I poured the lukewarm coffee. Mandy must have been here about twenty minutes before. I was wide awake with no hangover. I sipped the coffee again.

Layla did come back to the Schwartzes' cottage with me last night…but…?

Mandy waited for me inside the snack bar. The signage was a combination of hand-painted cardboard and ancient beer and soda neon signs. Some worked, some flickered, and some were just filled with dust, dead. By chance or design, the snack bar, like the rest of the resort, had a neglected fifties feel.

Mandy waved me over to her table as soon as I opened the screen door.

I approached her table and noticed the vacant chair next to her had a large white towel draped over back of the red vinyl and chrome. Perhaps she was having coffee with a friend or—

Before another thought came, she was up from the table and snuggled next to me, her arm around my waist, her left breast, the good girl as she call it, was stuck between my right arm and back. As I tried to move, her fingers found the inside of my wrap around towel. She arched her feet so she could whisper in my ear.

"We have to get you relaxed today, you know that don't you?"

As she spoke, her hand left my waist and moved down my butt until she reached the edge of my towel. Her hand crept under the towel and began to stroke my bare ass.

"Ken Boy, Nancy sent you here to relax. You remember how to relax, don't you?"

I tried to move. She anticipated it. Her right hand shot down the front of my towel.

Her naked thighs trapped my leg and she began to squeeze. I took a hard step forward. The vice that held onto my leg was released. The hands inside my towel were gone, along with my towel. Mandy walked causally to her table with my towel held over her head. She righted herself in the chair and invited me to sit down by waving her index figure toward her nose.

I looked around the small snack bar and realized that we were alone. I placed my hand in front of my exposed crotch.

Mandy spoke again. "You know, Ken Boy, you're kind of an anomaly. You have small hands but you have a big cock."

I wanted to run back to the cottage but that would mean running naked through the resort.

"Ken Boy, get your bare ass over here now!" The voice was like a mocking mother's scold.

I walked over to her table, pulled out a chair across from my tormentor.

Mandy shook her head no.

"Sorry, Big Boy, but you gotta sit over here cause here is the towel and you can't sit bare-assed anywhere here in the resort."

She anticipated my next move, wrapping her hand firmly around the towel in the vacant chair. I moved quickly around the table, sat on the towel, and scooted as close to the table as I could. I placed my left hand over my man parts.

"Kinda wish you'd gone on that diet hey, Big Boy?"

"Why are you callin' me Big Boy?"

"Cause I never seen you naked before."

"Okay, what's the game?"

Mandy's voice became serious and her face turned from mirth to scorn.

"There's no game. I'm trying to get you to relax so you can do some work, experience what your friend, Nancy wanted you to."

"She's my agent, not my friend," I shot back.

"Boy, you are a cold son of a bitch, aren't you?"

"No, it's just everyone here assumes that Nancy Schwartz and I were a thing or had something going. It was just business, honest."

"So you're not a hard ass after all?" she replied.

"Hey, you tell me. Your hands were all over my ass a few minutes ago."

"I was only trying to prove a point."

"And the point?"

"Very simple. Your first naked experience is not the end of the world. You're not gonna get arrested. And, as you found out, you're not automatically going to produce massive wood."

I interrupted. "Oh, really! What makes you a specialist on human anatomy?"

A smile crossed Mandy's face. Her eyebrows arched like a light bulb coming on.

"Okay, Big Boy, here's the deal. You get a hard-on right now under the table, and I'll give you a hundred bucks. No, better yet, I'll give you a hundred bucks and a blow job. I just have to make it more interesting. I give you a hundred bucks, a blow job, and I'll swallow. So, whadda ya say?"

We both sat in silence for a moment.

Mandy's hand shot under the table and groped my dick.

"Look, Big Boy, I won't question your credentials so please don't call mine into question. Deal?"

"Deal...with one caveat."

"Whatever, Big Boy."

"That's it. I will not question your carnal knowledge of the human anatomy or sexuality if you will quit calling me Big Boy."

"I liked Ken Boy better anyway. Deal."

The conversation turned to my day's work. Mandy was good enough to have a quiet work area set up for me next to the snack shop and in the shade. She had Jerry, the handyman, rig some extension cords in case I needed to recharge my laptop.

"You know, we seldom ever see people working around here. Real work, anyway. Don't be offended if folks stop by and ask what you're doing."

"Tell you what," I replied, "there's nothing as boring as doing rewrites and final edits. The interruptions will be welcomed."

Mandy shoved her chair back and stood up next to me. She mentioned something about a work schedule and was about to excuse herself.

"Before you go," I said, "I just wanted to thank you for the coffee this morning. And, by the way, how did you know when Layla left my cottage?"

"First, always call the place The House or you'll have the natives up your ass for committing a sacrilege. And I saw her leave when I was doing my morning patrol duty."

"You know, nothing happened." I explained.

"After seeing your performance this morning I'm sure that's true."

We both laughed.

"But seriously," I continued. "She asked if she could spend the night and I told her yes. She walked in and went to Nancy's bedroom and fell asleep."

Mandy looked directly into my eyes before she said anything. I expected a sharp retort but was relieved her eyes weren't too serious.

"Ken Boy, nothing ever happens with Layla, well hardly ever," she said softly.

"What's her story?"

"Since we both have some work to do this morning, I'll give you the *Reader's Digest* version...Layla is in her late thirties. She was married once briefly and the guy took off. Her parents and relatives go back a long way in Florida. She does have Indian blood on both sides. Her first love has always been her horses. People claim that she likes to sleep in the barn some nights just to be next to them."

Mandy paused and I was about to tell her how Layla had mentioned to me that she did indeed sleep in the barn, but I decided to keep it to myself.

"Both Layla and her husband were horse people—rodeos, horse shows, trail rides, you name it, they were involved. When Layla got pregnant, she slowed down for a little bit. After the baby girl, she literally made one of them papoose carriers so he could take the baby riding with her and her husband. You've heard of kids growing up around horses, well this kid grew up on horses.

"Layla's daughter was about four years old when they were on an overnight in the Everglades, one of those where you trailer the horses in and everyone rides all day and you camp at night. They took the little girl with them. She took turns riding with Mom then Dad. At night they built campfires and traded bullshit stories with the other riders. The little girl slept between Layla and her husband in a small tent. They woke up in the morning and the little girl was gone."

Mandy's eyes filled with tears. She stopped momentarily to collect herself.

"Yeah, the kid was gone. There was a massive manhunt and the story made the all the news. They never found the kid and supposedly Layla has not been quite right since. Speculators say a gator, panther, or something wild must have dragged the little girl off.

"The marriage ended a few months after the child disappeared. Seems parents blame each other when something like that happens. Add to that, cops tried to get the parents to confess or roll over on the other one. It was a mess. After the husband left, Layla sought out companionship.

"She'd hang out at bars, pick up men. Like with you, sleeping with her didn't necessarily mean having sex. Some of the locals got a little rough with her a time or two. Her parents got her the job at Butt Crack a few years back and she's been here ever since, seven days a week. Most of us are used to having her show up naked on our couches or hammocks. As you may have noticed, we don't have much use for locks here."

Mandy got up again. "If you got any more questions there gonna hafta wait till I'm done with my chores."

Mandy showed me my new office, a patio table with an umbrella, a metal chair, and a bright orange extension cord held down by a giant clear glass ashtray.

"You got shade, electric, and full view of the path to the pool. I suggest you take a dip every couple of hours or you'll melt."

I retrieved my briefcase from The House and walked back to my patio office. On the way I was greeted no less than twenty times by the natives wishing me "Good Morning" and "Hope y'all are enjoying yourself." Even the Yankees used the expression "y'all." It sounded threatening when delivered by a Brooklyn accent.

Once settled, I opened the package containing the edited version of my latest book.

Expecting the worst, I ripped opened the large manila envelope. I looked over the front page and saw the familiar red print distinct to Nancy.

Not bad stuff! I have marked up some questionable grammar and you need to do some minor rewrites. All in all, a good work. If you are in Florida, it should take you two days, given some of the diversions that are common to Lake Paradise.

Nancy

PLUS - Where in hell did you learn your grammar?"

Nancy and I had a running battle with grammar. I tried to explain that attending six to seven different grammar and high schools, some schools twice, I had some lifelong gaps in grammar usage. She loved my dialogue but hated my verb tenses.

A smile crossed my face. She bad-mouthed the work to make sure I would get on the rewrites and corrections as soon as possible. She knew I would probably follow her suggestion and go to Florida. After last night's bar talk with the boys, I realized she wanted me to learn something about her past—but why the urgency? Was she really dying?

Nancy was right about taking longer in Florida. As my laptop clicked out rewrites and grammar corrections, the random citizens of Lake Paradise made it over to my "office." After last night, it seemed as if the entire place knew I had a "close personal relationship" with the Schwartzess and thought Nancy and I the best of friends. So much for spreading gossip in a nudist camp. Mo, Pete, and Mike must have kept their hunch about Nancy's health to themselves. No one asked about her.

Mandy stopped by and asked, "Ken Boy, you need anything?"

"A little peace and quiet would be nice."

"You are the resident celebrity this week, so it goes with the territory. But I'll spread the word that you're deep in thought and you need your quiet."

"Appreciate it, thanks."

"Well, you owe me, and I plan to collect later. Understood, stud muffin?" She winked and blew me a kiss.

Mandy was true to her word and the procession of old timers did stop. A young redhead came by to take a lunch order. She was clothed in tight shorts and a Florida State t-shirt. I was disappointed that she wasn't naked.

After lunch, Mandy came by to tell me it was time to take a break and get in the water.

"How's the book going, Ken Boy?"

"Okay, really. It's going okay. At this rate, I should be out of here in a couple of days."

"Seems like you're in a hurry to leave our little paradise here."

I sensed some hurt in her voice. "No, not that I want to get out of here. Rewrites are a bitch and getting them done and done quickly is every writer's dream. I thought I had a bunch of stuff, but I am flying through all of Nancy's demands."

"Get your ass in the water before you melt down. Don't forget to read the pool rules before you get in."

"One question?"

"Shoot, Ken Boy."

"How come the little hottie wears clothes?"

Mandy gave me a hard stare before answering. "You mean Chloe?"

"I don't know her name, but she's got on the hot pants and tight Florida State t-shirt."

"Hot pants! Jesus Christ, I haven't heard that word in a long time. How old are you, man?"

"She was hot and the shorts are tight—what else do you want me to call them?"

"Well I think the kids call them Daisy Dukes, but if you're interested, she gets off at four fifteen. The pool usually fills up because ole Chloe likes to take a dip. If you read the rules, 'No swimsuits allowed.'"

"Why does the pool fill up at four fifteen?"

"You've heard of 'Miller Time'—well when Chloe takes her afternoon dip it's 'Chloe Time.' Every low-hangin' dick in this place comes watch her strip down and take a few laps. Let's be honest, Ken Boy, she is the hottest thing in the resort—next to me of course! And once you get over the one tit thing, I am not that bad."

Mandy was an attractive woman and she had a very nice body. "Mandy, you are a beautiful woman, period."

"You're either a gentleman or you're trying to get down my pants. Since I'm not wearin' pants, I'll go with the gentleman thing."

As predicted, the pool did fill up a little after four. As soon as Chloe stripped down I realized what the fuss was about. Chloe walked up to a vacant chair, pulled her top off, and wiggled out of her tight shorts. She had a sleek, athletic body. With a few stretches she dove into the pool. Five laps later she was out. She put her t-shirt over her shoulder, clutched her shorts in her hand, and left the pool area.

As soon as she left, the old timers resumed their daily routines, wanderinged off to their trailers and golf carts.

The next few days were much like the days before. Write, break for meals, go to the Butt Crack and have a few drinks. What also became routine was Layla coming to the cottage and falling asleep in Nancy's old bedroom.

The Boys gave me a wide path, didn't talk much other than to say hello or good morning. I asked Mandy about it and she mentioned that they knew the inevitable was coming soon and they didn't want to interfere with my writing.

The rewrites and edits went quickly. By day three, I realized my stay at Lake Paradise was soon to end.

Other than Chloe Time, I got used to the nude routine. After a few days, I didn't really notice the nudity, save Mandy coming up behind me and abusing my back with her breast.

"Well, Ken Boy, is today the day you break your vow of chastity?" Before walking away, she pat my bare ass and whispered, "Later, baby, later."

It was Mandy's golf cart that raised my head up from my laptop. She pulled up next to the fence. Absent was her usual banter as she walked up to me with the brown UPS envelope that covered her vacant right breast.

For the first time Mandy looked serious. Her smile faded into a straight face.

"Mandy, what's with the long face?"

"You got this package from a law firm in New York. It was delivered UPS. Seems those people don't want their boys and girls sunning around with a bunch of nudies.

"Anyways, I was in the gate house when the truck came. Mo was there too. He took a look at the return address and said, 'She's gone, our little Nancy's gone.'

"'How the fuck do you know she's gone by looking at an envelope?' I asked him. Harv and Marie used to joke about the Jew-Italian thing with the guys—their law firm in the city was Cohen and Giuliani. The Jew and Italian lawyers are the guys that handled their estate. Now they are handling little Nancy's.

"Mo handed the envelope back to me and said, 'Tell Ken we'll have a ceremony tomorrow morning.'"

Mandy handed me the UPS package. I ripped open the brown envelope and took out a typed letter from Cohen and Giuliani.

Dear Ken,

It is with our deepest regret that we inform you of the untimely death of Ms. Nancy Schwartz. Ms. Schwartz passed on Tuesday evening at her private residence on Second Avenue.

In accordance with New York State law, she needed to appoint an executor of her estate.

Over the last two weeks, Ms. Schwartz has made a number of contacts with our office requesting that you be named executor.

Again, upon Ms. Schwartz's request, we have enclosed a personal letter addressed to you to be delivered upon her death.

Please contact our office at your earliest possible convenience to review Ms. Schwartz's estate.

Sincerely,

Barry I. Cohen, Esq.

I refolded the letter and replaced it then retrieved a plain white envelope with the one word on the front written in longhand.

Ken

I handed Mandy the UPS envelope. "Is Moe right?" she asked respectfully.

I nodded and proceeded to rip open the letter.

"Dear Kenny," the letter began in the same perfect long hand that appeared on the outside of the envelope.

If you are reading this, it means I am dead. Oh boy, you can't imagine how many books I rejected for opening with that statement. But let's be honest—I am dead, and to put it in very simple terms: you are a very rich man. But, and there are always buts, you have to spend some time earning your new fortune.

I have left the heavy stuff to the lawyers. They are good people, but they are lawyers. And as my dad and mom always said, after we die the only thing the lawyers have to remember us by is our money.

My simple request for you is to act as my agent after my death. I have written over fifteen novels and a bunch of short stories. Your job will be to work with my publishers and make sure the books get out on a regular basis (once a year at least).

You know I have peddled other people's schlock for my entire adult life, and now, after death, it is my turn to kick some ass. I thought about publishing while I was living, but I really could not have stood up to the ghoul watch that would have followed me through life. You know, a collection of my pictures as my condition deteriorates... And of course, the tabloids would have had a field day with the "East Side Golem." Yeah, I've known about my moniker for a long time.

I have also left you some hard cash, a lot, my building on Second Avenue, and that house you're staying in at Lake Paradise.

Ken, I did not have the courage to talk to you about my life and planning my death. I thought it would be best that you discover me from people who knew my family and me in my past life.

Take care and have a good life.

By the way, you are a decent man—simple as that.

Take care.

Your Agent for Life,

Nancy

I reached for the UPS envelope Mandy was holding.
"Are you okay, Ken Boy?" she asked.
"I don't know. A lady I hardly knew just made me a multi-millionaire."
I didn't deserve this gift. I felt guilty about the bad things I'd said. Mostly I felt sad that someone like Nancy had to go through life battling a catastrophic illness, all the while making a name for herself in the publishing world, earning millions. For what? To die alone?